T0365048

THE EYE OF THE WHALE

BRUCE BENSON

authorHOUSE®

AuthorHouse™ UK
1663 Liberty Drive
Bloomington, IN 47403 USA
www.authorhouse.co.uk
Phone: 0800.197.4150

Published by AuthorHouse 05/18/2016

ISBN: 978-1-5246-3478-0 (sc)
ISBN: 978-1-5246-3479-7 (e)

Print information available on the last page.

Any people depicted in stock imagery provided by Thinkstock are models, and such images are being used for illustrative purposes only. Certain stock imagery © Thinkstock.

This book is printed on acid-free paper.

PART ONE

CHAPTER 1

The aftermath of yet one more International Whaling Conference was being cleared up in the building. Posters and bits of paper littered the floor. Chairs had been overturned by over zealous activists, sick of hearing the same old spiel on whaling quotas. Many of these die hard activists had campaigned for years to end this barbarism. There was even some blood at the front where security staff had grappled with some who simply could not take the latest washing of the hands decision to continue whaling for scientific purposes. Some journalists were snapping their hi- tech cameras and some leading news stations were doing live bulletins.

As the crowd dissipated a lone figure is seen standing at the back, dressed in blue jeans, donkey jacket and grey woollen hat. He was about 5 foot ten inches with brown hair and whiskers. He had some sort of trekking boots on. He was stood there in some sort of mesmeric trance, for he could not take all that he had witnessed in. It would not register. Sonny Preston was his name. He had been a leading anti whaling campaigner for the past three years. Highly intelligent he thought that a ban was finally on the cards, and that all this false pretence by Japan, Norway and Iceland to hunt whales for scientific reasons would be over. They got away with it time and time again. When, he thought, would mankind leave these giants of the seas and time itself to swim the oceans in peace.

The place was Reykjavik Iceland, June 2015. How strange he thought that even in the 21century, mankind could still not sort out its problems. And that for all of religion and all of the wars, whales had lived for millions of years. It was daunting for Sonny to think that man would soon kill everything on the planet in an insanity that not even Dante could dream up.

Man with his awesome weapons of mass destruction that seem of little use but which gobbled up budgets and the best brains in the world. Food factory farming was now routinely talked of. Even whale farming was openly on the agenda, put forward by the Japanese smooth negotiators. Cars were everywhere. Litter was strewn across the planet and oceans, without a care in the world. Even man's attempt to investigate space had come up with little except expert robotic warfare. Sonny envisaged the ultimate battle soon, where a new breed of robots would terminate, as in the Arnold Swarzenigger movies, human beings. The world was heading for apocalypse and there was little it seemed that could be done. It was quite terrifying to behold. Sonny was 35 years old. As of yet he had no children. Indeed he thought the world no fit place for children.

It was he thought the final conference for him. He had other plans. Big plans. As of yet private, but that which would rock the world to the core. He saw himself now, after this final insult with whale factory farms, as some sort of earthly messiah come to rid the world of man's insatiable greed and lust for all things material.

A cleaner bumped into him, bringing him out of his reveries.

She was Philippino, or something like that he mused.

"You nowhere to go," she asked innocently.

He thought for a while then said, "The world can seem so sick at times, I wonder if there is a place where anybody can go."

"Well, I know what you mean. Me a cleaner and just look at this mess."

"Yes, I must apologise. We must tell our friends to be more respectful but things get heated."

"You people see yourselves as green, yet you cannot dispose of your own litter"!

"I know, it is terrible." And with that he turned around and walked towards the exit.

Outside the harsh northern sun of Iceland struck him full in the face and he squinted. Getting his bearings he turned right along the main street the Aolstraati and looked for a coffee shop. There were dispersing crowds and police along the pavements. He wondered if all of these demonstrations ever achieved anything. He saw up ahead a cafe named the Pink Flamingo. And there was a sign of the bird outside above the shop's entrance. In he went and got a few stares from the native Icelandic people who perhaps saw him as one of them eco leftist nutters who had caused trouble at the whaling conference. It always amazed Sonny just how indifferent the masses were to whales and to life on this planet more generally. Wars were everywhere. Weapons. Giant gas guzzling cars and planes. People lived like there was no tomorrow and just did not seem to care about the planet.

The assistant behind the counter knew immediately that he was not local. Sonny looked out of place but he needed to gather his thoughts. Sit by himself and ponder on not just the future of whales but of the direction his future life would take for he had plans. Plans that he felt would finally reorder the mayhem that this planet had become. He noticed that on a rack were some internationalist newspapers. He briefly looked at the menu and ordered the ubiquitous Cappuccino. How he wished he could be different as western cafes were as much a part of the culture of decadence as pollution itself. Starbucks. Macdonalds. Café Neros et cetera. Waste. Money. Capitalism. He had never been a messiah type figure in his mind. Once upon a time he had been a top marine biologist working out of UCLA researching into many things but the corruption of the cosmetic industry proved too much. When he had finally put in a complaint about the manner in which the Japanese carried out an annual cull of Dolphins off a bay in Japan, he found himself ostracised from high academia. His career in ruin he became a drifter. Moving from one town to another, slowly latching onto the environmental cause. With an IQ of around 160, he could at times find life frustrating. He had hoped to go onto be a professor in marine biology but now he read largely 'green' literature and more left wing radicalised books. He had been placed in a psychiatric ward for a while when he had got into trouble over make up being tested on dolphin skins. But he knew the score in today's world. He knew that there was a glamorous artistic elite that live for beauty and perfection. But he had fallen in love with the cause of the whale, figuring it to a super being that should not be allowed to die out or be researched upon like it its planet was a giant concentration camp. He felt that cosmetics could be tested in other ways. Besides every time the Japanese government issued statements that it needed to whale for 'scientific reasons' he felt the word scientific was being abused. Science should be about doing good and about invention for good causes. It seemed Capitalist thinking was still the driving force of the world. A world that sent man to the moon in 1968 yet still in 2011 had gas guzzling giant cars that rendered huge tracts of the atmosphere non breathable. He picked up a tray, placed the huge Cup of Cappuccino on it and selected a cake covered in pink icing. 20 euros. He paid the cashier and moved to a seat by the window so he could watch people go by. Just like his life was becoming a journey to nothing he thought of all those protestors who had made their way to Iceland, largely for no reward at all.

Iceland seemed such a modern type of country, although with a small population the capital was resplendent, with four by four vehicles everywhere. Somewhat bizarrely, Iceland prided itself on green technology such as electricity generation from geezers. Yet for Sonny, the plaintive fact was that the country felt the need to assert a type of macho pride as it still whaled. He saw a couple of hippy type girls carrying a placard,

"Kill the whalers." Sonny was thinking that it was the green movement in general that appeared to have a kind of "nice" non violent image. Whale protestors were seen as mainly peaceful types who never engaged in terrorism. That was soon to end as Sonny had finally made plans, He had reached the end titration point of a long journey of self introspection. He had nothing materialistic in life. No fixed home. No girlfriend or car. No ties to allow him to live the life that most people on earth seemed to want. Certainly the Icelandic government had created a modern city in all respects, even though the winters could be rotten. He guessed he always knew the outcome of this year's commission, as it was by now routine. Okay a moratorium had been won earlier in the century as stocks were of pristine whales sank to all time lows, but he knew that this 'scientific' angle was annoying everyone with connections to the safeguarding of the environment. But governments were so powerful. He knew that SOMETHING concrete and violent had to be done to finally rid the world of the scourge of modern day whaling practices. Even as he thought of the word 'scientific' he dreaded to conjure up what was going on some of those huge Whale Factory Ships.

As he sighed in the sunlight streaming through the window, he was strangely happy that that there were others who shared his sentiments with displaying this placard. Maybe he should go and shake their hands, but he did not need to. He had put his plans into operation. He had thought long and hard about what to do and decided that he would use his awesome intelligence to save these giants of time. Beasts that were the masters of the aqua sphere in all that it represented and also masters of time. Just like the greatest human minds that ever lived, such as Albert Einstein, Alexander Solzhenitsyn, Roger Penrose, and Stephen Hawkin to name a few thought on the complexities of astrophysics, maybe the whale spent much of its time to musing on time and space. It was one of the Japanese Prime Ministers, Isako Suzuki who had released a statement to the world saying that the whale was merely a fish. A fish. To Sonny man had to invent diving suits, aqua lungs, submarines and sophisticated radar techniques to get about in the water, whilst some whales could alter their shape as they dived to below 500 meters without getting the infamous bends like humans. When Sonny sometimes switched on television to watch wildlife programmes he was always fascinated at the sight of humpbacks breeching the water and twisting. He thought maybe it was a sign that they were tired of living on this tiny planet where man brutalised all. Or maybe it was some kind of plea to a God out there in the universe. Either way soon, if all his plans went well, whaling would cease and there would be respect for everything Environmental. No huge farms of cattle for the Macdonald's fast burger industry, and definitely no more whaling. He wanted to see that whale stocks would grow to good levels once again, although with the amount of ships and military utilising the seas he doubted if this goal would now be achievable. But it was readily achievable to prevent whaling taking place ever again. If only he actually knew what went on in these factory ships. Sadly the instruments of government kept this top secret. We the masses were never going to find out what the word 'scientific' really meant.

He put two spoons of sugar from the bowl on the ultra clean white table into his cappuccino and stirred the cup. Sugar, what a huge industry that was too. People were obese everywhere with burgers and other fast foods readily available. Although extremely intelligent he was a pragmatist. He could of course forget about sugar and the simple everyday pleasures of the so called free and democratic west. He knew in his heart that he should be courting some nice girl and settling down with children, because that was what evolution was all about. Maybe when his 'mission' was over he would reengage the real world. But for now he had only one goal on his mind to save these monsters of the deep from such a fateful death sentence as 'scientific whaling', the loophole that the whalers hid behind. And for so long. But this was going to end. The more he thought the more determined he became. He knew that there may be casualties but although he would try to be a bit like Robin Hood or ironically Arnold Shwarzenigger in Terminator Two whereby he did not kill anyone, he knew that reality of any sort was vastly different than science fiction. He was not writing a science fiction book. Someone had to make a decision and he had made up his mind once and for all. And he knew that he must not attract attention to himself as his plans developed.

He picked up the pink cake and savoured the moment.

"Better than a Big Mac", he mused.

He left for his hotel some 30 minutes later. It was not far off the main street. In he went, though noting he was not a well dressed foreigner on holiday. Just as he did so he was met by a lovely girl in dungarees.

"Hi, I saw you at the conference. I am not staying here but I was wondering now that I have bumped into you what did you think."

"Well, it seems that it is the usual bullshit."

"I know. If I had my way I would blow the fucking whalers off the face of the earth."

At first he was struck by the violence of this good looking girl, but then he saw just how passionate she was in her look.

"I know how you feel."

Then the girl said,

"What you doing now?"

"I am going to have a warm shower, so please excuse my decadence. Say how would you like to come to my room and have a talk about the Whaling conferences of the world. And maybe a drink?"

She looked down at her feet and seemed a bit tentative.

"Life is generally a bit of a big bullshit. I know it's a nice hotel but yes, sure, but I only drink soft drinks."

"Me too, but we could have a tea or coffee if you'd like. I am her only tonight then have to go Amsterdam for some important business."

"Okay."

So they got the elevator up to the third floor, room 35. Sonny asked her for her name after introducing himself, to which she said,

"Tanya."

"That's nice. You sound Canadian."

"Yes, Vancouver. I sort of live semi-rough there with my dogs. She got out a photograph showing Tanya outside a caravan with two Red Setters. There was no man in the shot.

"Me, I am American, Los Angeles. Would you believe it I once used to be a marine biologist at the University of California."

"Wow. What went wrong"

"I fell fowl of the authorities. Now I drift around attending green causes with whales something I deeply feel about."

They sat down in his room and Tanya noticed the quite luxurious room and flat screen television.

"I will ring down for coffee." Said Sonny facing Tanya.

"I will just have orange or whatever they do here in Iceland."

"Yes I am not gemmed up on the local culture, but it seems such a modern city."

Tanya somewhat ironically added,

"You would think that such a place that is well into green technology would not feel the need to whale."

"I suppose the only bonus is that because the conference was held here maybe some top writers will contrast that fact. You know how the country should be moving forward with the green movement."

"One problem is, the sort of censorship of the whole environmental debate, and how slow things seem to progress."

"Yes I know. And the manner in which leading governments put it to the back burner. Wars seem to be fine. Money no object there. But with these gentle beasts of time and nature it seems they have no right to live," added Sonny reflectively.

The drinks came and it seemed Iceland had some such juice delicacy. Sonny although just having had a cappuccino, and a giant one at that preferred another coffee as was the general way with Americans. "Its hard", he finally said. "So hard."

"In what way do you especially mean." Tanya added inquisitively.

At this point Sonny got to thinking of the remark mentioned when they first met. "Blow the fuckers off the face of the earth."

She could immediately see the pain on the face of Sonny.

"Well. Can I trust you?" He figured that he could." We've only just met I know, but it seems to me that the environmental movement always pussy foots about. We are known as the peaceful sorts who accept all the dictates of modern governments. From my point of view it is time some of us stood up and got counted on the world stage. I have been thinking for quite some time to strike at the heart of some governments, and ram home the message that Whales were not placed here on this lonely earth to be researched upon by man. That this planet was not meant for that purpose. I am not a preacher or anything like that but I am prepared to take direct action. Just like a Nelson Mandella-type figure."

Tanya was captivated by the good looking Sonny and his stance. Sonny continued,

"Obviously I cannot do things all by myself. I would need some others who they themselves would be willing to be sort of martyrs. I am not crazy or anything. I am not an eco-nutter as some journalists have described so ardently at times. I do not hear voices guiding me, but just think for one moment what goes on, on one of those huge Japanese Factory ships."

Tanya winced. "I dread to think."

"And for what? Cosmetics today do not need to research on animals it has been proven beyond all doubt."

"Well, the governments keep quiet on this for sure. So whatever it is must be top secret."

"Sonny thought a bit longer before tentatively saying,

"How would you like to join me. To help me "Blow the fuckers" off the face of the earth."

Tanya realised that her words had been pretty violent, but she did not herself realise what this could mean. Not knowing exactly what this enigmatic Sonny had up his sleeve., however she was 100% behind the idea, thinking similarly that the green movement had reached an impasse in that being goody goody was getting nowhere.

She added thoughtfully,

"I agree with you. Enough is enough. Someone has to lead the way else the planet will be one giant whale farm for burgers and dog food."

Sonny was pleased and in his own way rather shyly shook hands with Tanya.

"You do realise what this entails," he said. There will have to be secrecy. Violence. Weapons and cunning and guile. There will be governmental agencies set up to deal with the likes of us."

"Yes, I know there will be a lot of sacrifice, but I already feel better having met you. It has been a privilege indeed."

They both smiled feeling that they were meant to be destined to save the whales.

"So what now," eventually Tanya interrupted the silence,

"There is much, much to do. I intend to recruit two more people. I have put adverts out in the media. I am looking for people who fear little and are committed to this cause. In fact that is part of the reason that I am going to Amsterdam to meet two people. I had also hoped to hire a female but you seem ideal. Together we can save these whales from extinction and much pain. Just like the Baader Meinhoffs and Che Gavaras of this world we can alter the destiny of humanity. The time is right for this. What do you think?" Sonny finally added.

"You know. It sounds fantastic. I have just been waiting for the opportunity to do something terroristic, as I too, had reached the conclusion that being goody two shoes got one nowhere. I know it is a bit drastic but it has been proven that terrorism achieves much of its aim. Look at the I.R.A. Many of their operatives are free and mingle with the elite of the political world. It is as if terrorism earns you respect. However, for me it is not respect that I want. I want an end to the suffering of these beasts. And the only logical conclusion to draw is that to achieve this some sort of terrorism is needed." Tanya broke off in her vexed state.

"I know", Sonny stated with both conviction and wisdom." But it is not respect we are after. There has to be the ultimate message that there is more to this world than animal factory farming or gas guzzling automobiles. And that as the world's leaders seem incapable of doing anything in this direction save toadying to big business, I see no reason why the public at large will not help us. But we need to be very careful in our planning and tactics. If we get discovered early on then the suffering of the whale will go on. Can you come with me to Amsterdam tomorrow to meet these two people. There is probably time and room to still book on the British Airways flight. Or have you got somewhere else to go?"

"Well, I have my two Red Setters in Vancouver who will miss me and one question I need to ask is how are we going to get the money that we will need to buy equipment and flights and so such. To do anything takes a lot of money these days."

"I have thought much about the way to proceed. I guess we will need a minimum of 50 million pounds or more in dollars. But I have some friends still who are working in the higher echelons of finance. I have been told that to hack into the accounts of Macdonalds for instance would double our message. Or even a world bank. It can be done. But first we need to be a team and get to know each other. I put an advert in several of the worlds press and I have whittled the list of people down to two. We meet at the hotel Capitool near the train station."

"Sounds cool. I have been to Amsterdam before with its liberal ideas on drugs. Also it has a very active red light district."

"Yes, but it is relatively easy to get lost there. And of course we can see the sights. And the bonus is that many arms dealers operate there, so we can buy equipment. One never knows for sure what will happen with my plans but Amsterdam is a good place to start. I can lay out basic ideas. But one goal that I am particularly keen on is to take out one of these giant Factory Ships."

"Wow. That would be fantastic as long as there were no live whales on."

"Yes, I was thinking maybe even then it would still would be a good idea because we do not know what they are doing inside one of those things."

"It won't be easy getting aboard for a start and moving around without speaking Japanese for example will make it extra hard. But I see with detailed planning and with the right people we can be successful. It is daring and adventurous but it HAS to be done. I see no other way round the problems of today's materialistic world."

"Like you say security will have to be tight and the many governments have the resources to stop us. But I was at the University of California so there are some top computer geeks that I know who can do things you cannot dream of with computers."

"What about green campaigners in other countries like Japan?", enquired Tanya trying to add to the debate.

"Well, the problem there is that many Japanese too, think of whales as being mere fish like delicacy for eating, but there are contacts should we need them. Maybe places to stay and that sort of thing. But there is a strong Japanese Green movement."

"But getting drawings of a Whaling ship et cetera they could prove helpful with the language."

"Yes. What we will do is sleep on it and then when we meet up with these two others tomorrow we can go into things with a little more detail. You must be tired now. Where are you staying, by the way, continued Sonny.

"Oh, there is a small hostel type place on the waterfront. It does not cost much and you get to meet people like yourself. There were many youngsters from all over Europe staying there."

"Well do not tell anyone of our talk. The strictest silence is needed. The police have extensive networks of informers."

"Do not worry. There is no way I'm going to 'blow' this, if you will excuse the pun."

They both momentarily saw the humour, but it was short lived as the harsh realities of modern day precision whaling sunk in.

After a brief pause which seem to last for eternity, Sonny got up from his very comfortable chair and said,

"I will give you my phone number so you can ring me to let me know if you can get on the flight to Amsterdam."

"No problems. How long were you planning on staying in Amsterdam by the way, "asked Tanya before leaving the hotel room.

"I thought of two nights initially to sort of feel out things. It could be longer. I guess it depends on what these people are like."

"OK, I ring later. Bye. And off she went to the hostel. Sonny looked through the hotel window and watched her amble down the street. He had met someone who seemed to fit the bill perfectly. "Blow the fuckers off the face of the earth." He was not going to forget that phrase because it said everything there was to say about what he had planned.

Sonny decided to rest for a short while. He switched on the flat screen to catch the news headlines. After fiddling with the remote he found an English news station and per chance it briefly mentioned the crowd trouble inside the conference. Then a picture of a whale being harpooned. This made Sonny wince, yet also hardened his steely reserve to engage in what he knew would be considered as terrorism. He knew that in his heart many die hard greens would never forgive him for what he had planned no matter the outcome as many were peaceful people. They did not like to be classed as eco nutters or environmental terrorists. Sonny had spent some time in a secure psychiatric unit for getting involved with the back room politics of the huge power house of the world wide cosmetic industry. He had refused to do research into mammalian aquatic skin technology thinking that there was both no need and that life on this planet meant more than vanity for the beautiful. It had not been pleasant being incarcerated on mind warping drugs but it had hardened him to reality. If they can do that to me, a highly educated person what was to stop these researchers treating the entire planet as their own private backyard to do what they pleased. It had been proven that cosmetics could be tested or researched on by other means.

When he had festered in the top secure psychiatric unit in Nevada, along side some quite seriously disturbed people known as sociopaths or psychopaths he thought of all his planning for the ultimate terrorist outrage. He too had heard of the war to end all wars. But he was thinking more of the terror plots to end all terror plots. A new way of thinking and working on the planet. To do this would require more than what the I.R.A. and the P.L.O. used to get up to. Make no mistake, although Sonny had been diagnosed with a personality disorder he was no fool. He knew that governmental heads were the best targets or company directors of cosmetic companies. And then the finale: the destruction of a whaling ship beamed live to the world's media. It would be audacious. Brave. Daring. It would require tremendous planning, cunning, and a dedicated group who did not believe in violence for violence sake but who had genuine reasons for helping these gentle beasts of time. He had contacts in high academic circles and had found, in Tanya a formidable intelligence, and someone who would go all the way. Ideally none of them was to die but he knew the way things were. To be Robin Hood- like was all very well, but in practice it was something not achievable.

He switched off the television and lay back on his clean and comfy bed thinking before falling into a dreamy drowsy state. Meanwhile Tanya was back at the hostel. Nothing flashy there. Communal beds but it was very clean and modern in keeping with Reykjavik in general. She was talking to some people who too had been at the conference and they were all depressed.

"What can we do?" said a disgruntled bearded man of about 30 years of age, "it seems impossible. It is the same every time there is a meeting. Quotas and more scientific legal clauses and loopholes to continue their savage butchery."

Tanya listened intently to these people. Tanya too had been on many trips around the world to demonstrate. Although living semi homeless in a caravan near Vancouver with her dogs, she got about, but the authorities in Canada had labelled her a dyke, a fanatic who knew nothing of the world's problems. Whilst on the contrary she had studied English literature at the university of Vancouver and had good knowledge of the many issues involved in the world today. But whilst, like many of her fellow supporters care about stopping wars, she felt the whaling issue was all related. She felt that simply it demonstrated that governments were, in fact, incapable of running the planet and that this had a knock on effect around the planet. It seemed that the more educated you became the more the authorities saw you as dangerous. Where as in reality these people were the ones who should inherit the earth as it said in the bible. But she was not religious. Such people too had proven they could not run the planet. She was also thinking of Sonny and what intelligence he oozed. She felt somewhat elated that she could now be part of 'direct action', as it were to do something concrete. Although too, she never agreed with violence, she also had become hardened to the constant denial of these whales to freely swim about in the water, in unpolluted water free of research. She felt the planet was there for everyone to enjoy in its purist sense and felt that pollution could be solved if the politicians did their job. But they did not. Never, always toadying up to Big Business. And that reminded her. She went outside briefly to make a call free of anyone else's hearing range to the travel agents. To her disdain she was amazed that there was no way she could get on a plane to Amsterdam tomorrow. It seems that many people had come to this particular conference as there had been some optimism, now a false dawn it seemed, that whaling would be banned indefinitely. So demand for many flights had been huge and with Amsterdam being a pivotal place in the world as a freedom city it was too be expected that many green supporters came from there. She got through to directory enquiries and asked for the number for hotel Geyser Spring, amusing herself over the name. But it was certainly a modern hotel. Sonny was lucky she thought to be staying in such a place. But there was no trace of resentment. She was fully aware of the way things were. Besides it took great men to change or alter destiny and staying with those who took hash as many probably did in the hostel would get in the way of Sonny's plans. No she thought there was nothing pretentious about Sonny. He needed his room. His time to plan and think. She got the number and asked the switchboard to be put through to room 35. It took a while and she feared that he had gone out, but then the phone was picked up.

"Hello." She was relieved to hear his voice. "Sorry to disturb you its Tanya here. I cannot get to Amsterdam tomorrow. It seems all flights are fully booked. The travel agencies say they had never known a meeting as popular as this, and that they hoped there would be more such international meetings in their prestigious city. Maybe big business gets even bigger?" she sardonically said.

"Yes. It would seem so. We had whale watching off California which proved a success. Maybe some business whiz kid was marketing international whaling conferences. It would not surprise me what these Harvard graduates got up to. Yet maybe we can play them at their own game some day." He added in a contemplative manner.

"You've got your mind thinking again, Sonny. That's good. Well I am sorry I would love to meet these other two characters."

"Don't worry. Give me your number and address in Vancouver and I will reassess the way things should proceed. By the way you don't think these phones are being listened too by the government do you?" hastened Sonny to add.

"Well, I would not put anything past them, though they are so smug they think the environmentalists are done with," asserted Tanya.

"Yes, they do but I think we should veer on the safe side and maybe use some kind of code from now on. I read in some press releases that the authorities did not think that liberal minded environmentalists could have the resolve or resources to carry out any big acts of terror. On the news a while ago the fracas in the conference room where the many delegates from the different countries met was reported. It seems that liberal good natured people always get to be seen as rowdy trouble makers with long hair who smoke dope."

Tanya added, "They say evil never triumphs. Let's prove it finally."

To which Sonny thought." Did you say you had a degree Tanya?"

"Yes. English literature at the University of Vancouver."

"That may prove very useful for statements and such because you have given me an idea there. I'll have to go but I will get in touch as soon as I can."

Tanya looked at her phone thinking that Sonny was indeed mysterious. She thought rather ironically, "Goodness will finally triumph."

CHAPTER 2

We see a busy police department, with many computer terminals and people both sat and walking around. To one side were some self contained offices and in one was a man of around 50, hair well thinning, and of somewhat rotund features. He had his feet up on the desk and was talking into his cell phone. His name was Adolfo Heinlitz He came from some kind of Italian ancestry and had a dark complexion. He was animated in his discussion, as he talked with the head of Draxon pharmaceuticals of Japan.

"Yes, according to my contacts in the police in Iceland there were only minor skirmishes in the conference room."

"At the other end was a Japanese voice that although spoke English well still had the pronounced Japanese overtones." That's not what I heard. Sources tell me that real violence erupted when the final scientific quotas were agreed to take 500 whales of all classes each year."

"Yeah, but it was nothing our boys could not handle. Just relax it is hardly the Irish republican Army or anything. And it has successfully dispersed. And is over now. We've got all angles covered so there is unlikely to be any riots. Reykjavik is a clean modern city. The Icelandic president himself was on to me to make sure it was kept that way. He has been told that many businesses and plane flights were fully booked, which was a bonus for a country with such a small economy." Adolfo Heinlitz prided himself on being a top police officer.

"Well that is good to hear. But my corporation pays good money to prevent trouble and expects results," said the man from Draxon, a man called Suto Suzuki.

"And you have got what you want. You and other countries can continue whaling for your scientific reasons. You just leave any potential revolutionaries up to us. As far as I know there have been no traces of anyone wanting to get into terrorism. You know yourself that that Europe is no longer a hot bed of terrorism, like the I.R.A. or the Red Brigades of the 80's. There is no fight there. The main threat to world disorder today seems to come from the Islamic preachers of hate direction. And all our sources say no group or person came up on a computer scan."

"Well in that case, keep up the good work. I just thought I would call you because any violent incident or threats to our delegates should not go unpunished."

"They won't. The protagonists were some old die hards that get into a scrape every time there is a conference. They have no balls to do anything drastic, of that I assure you."

"Good. Good. Well next year we meet in Brazil, so that is likely to be a hotbed of unrest what with illegal logging et cetera. And the climate change fanatics they seem to get stronger every year."

"We have things under control. No-one especial popped under the radar. There are no more heroes anymore. Believe me Mr. Suzuki."

"Well, we never know. What about that character with the high Intelligence quotient what was his name?"

"Oh you mean Sonny Preston. He's an ex psychiatric case on medication. He was there but my sources said he got up to nothing, though I have not had a detailed report. Besides where would he get the resources from. This is not like Noraid financing terrorist training camps with millions of dollars. These people simply have not got the capability to do anything."

"Yes, I agree. But he is a very clever man. IQ. of over 170 and with an axe to grind as he feels both the Cosmetic industry and elements in the police stitched him up. He could be dangerous."

"Look if it makes you feel any better we will keep a watch on him for a while. We kept a low profile in Iceland as the government wanted no bad publicity in their country which strangely prides itself on the application of Green Technology."

"Yes, but there is a hard core that are only interested in the whaling angle and Iceland like Norway and us keep on whaling and soon people will be prying on our scientific research too much. We want it all kosher. No hiccups. No strange stories leaked to some journalists what we get up to."

"Well if you've got nothing to hide why worry. Or are you doing something which you know will get up the backs of some do- gooders."

"I cannot say. I am a spokesman for Draxon Pharmaceuticals Corporation. It is a major employer and researcher into new medications. Whilst many governments appreciate our hard work, there will always be those that cause problems, and that Sonny Preston has friends through his university days in high places. I would not put anything past his capabilities."

"We did not tap any phones this time. It can get costly keeping tabs on people. And there is a militant Islamic question too, which most governments are concerned with, as elections results depend on how they view all those plane bombings in America."

"Yes, but America is the leading power in the world, which no Japanese truly can stomach, and they are totally against whaling. They have whale watching holidays off California which, I am told, prove quite popular and lucrative. So it is not merely a question of a few nutters. America has brains and the technology to do almost anything. In the wrong hands any outrage can occur."

"Well, I am an experienced operative. I have contacts. Law enforcements agencies do not like the idea of terrorism and it is the duty of international police agencies to stop such threats. I will put a request in for a thorough appraisal of all that is going on in the world of the environmental movements on this planet. If something is stirring we will find out, but remember Japan is not squeaky clean. There are people who hate what you do there."

"Maybe, but they are few and far between. Japan generally is well policed. It is just that I never did trust Americans, they get into causes and see them through. They dropped H bombs and saved Europe in the Second world War. This Sonny Preston may see himself as some sort of super American environmentalist, with a mission to prove that American again leads the world. The Japanese must fight this American control of the world. It is our culture that is under threat. The Japanese premier has said as much. We Japanese used to have the economic miracle of all miracles but lately things have switched back to the Americans. But we lead the way in robotics. There is not much that I wish to add, Adolfo. Just remember you get paid well. We want no slip ups or incompetence."

"You worry to much. When my team has done the appraisal I will contact you, but I do not envisage any problems."

"Okay. See you then".

And the phone was disconnected leaving a smiling Adolfo to contemplate. He had not heard anyone talk of this Sonny guy for a couple of years, so he decided to look up his file on the computer.

He accessed via the secure codes of the system the Data Bases on Environmental Potentials. This was a list of people deemed to have the nous and capability to organise acts of wanton vandalism and terrorism. Adolfo was a man of pragmatism. He knew that theoretically these lists could contain thousands, as most of the colleges of the world were full of lefties and layabouts who seemed only interested in terrorism. And the Environmental movement had been an ever increasing area of surveillance. At first he could find nothing as he typed in Sonny Preston but then accessed another Data Base on those with psychiatric histories as Adolfo knew that he had problems with his old University. And there it was.

A picture of Sonny when he used to have a beard, with base ball cap looking resplendent at some college dinner.

Adolfo laughed to himself,

"Looks the typical leftie type drifter but then read the brief report.

"Sonny Preston, age 35. No children. No fixed abode. No known girlfriends.

"Probably Gay," thought Adolfo.

Sonny was regarded as a potential danger by a leading Psychiatrist in the United States. He had an intelligence Quotient of 160 and although interred for a year in a top secure mental hospital had on one occasion escaped. He was recaptured easily however, and completed his sentence which was two years. He had cracked up during his work, claiming that some Japanese company was spying o him and suggesting that he was not doing h is work as a marine research biologist adequately. Sonny had protested that he had got too close to what Japanese researchers were up to, and they did not like the fact. The authorities said that he simply became unwell and that needed treatment. Adolfo read on.

With the treatment completed it was felt that Sonny could now live as a normal human being as long as he stayed clear of all things Japanese. It seemed that he had a complex about some of the activities of the Japanese with reference to certain aquatic life forms. He was always to be considered a danger in the sprawling environmental movement, it seemed that he had dropped off the radar.

Then Adolfo bolted upright, as he read on.

Last seen only a few days ago at the International Whaling conference in Iceland. He was now clean shaven and had stayed in the hotel Geyser Spring, all by himself.

"Geyser Spring," shouted Adolfo, "fucking Geyser Spring. There's me working my arse of saving the public from terrorists and this clown is having a holiday in Iceland at a hotel called Geyser Spring, what's the world coming to. And what about my security team. Where was my report. This should have been flagged up. He got the phone to his assistant a miss Suzie Adams and when she picked up he blasted,

"What the fuck do I pay you for, Miss Adams. I have just had a big company on my neck about the recent international whaling conference at Iceland, and it turns out that that creep Sonny Preston turned up there. Where's my report? Why wasn't I kept informed.

I can lose my job over this. You must know how dangerous some of these eco loonies can be. And the leading governments and companies expect us to protect them from them.

"Er er I am sssorry Adolfo. I do not know what happened. I will look into things," stammered Suzie,

"Not only will you do that when you found out why it was not flagged you will sack the fucking geek involved. Do you understand?"

"Fully. I will get on to it right away," and Adolfo slammed the phone down.

Suzie was a bit flustered but smiled briefly as Adolfo and the terrorist surveillance unit did not know that she was a plant for Sonny. Sonny had wanted an informant in the unit to help him with his plans. It turns out Suzie had once, though totally unknown to anyone, been a supporter of an organisation called Friends of the Earth whilst at college in England, and Sonny who had been formulating his plans for a long time had found out about her and had asked if she would help. She was a computer graduate and would be of assistance. Sonny explained the risk that she would take but that if she really felt as she once did that whales and dolphins should be allowed to roam freely in the seas, she could still use her considerable computer skills but at the same time do the environment some good. Suzie whose father was a highly known freemason had no difficulty obtaining the position although tactful not to let it be known that she wheedled her father into obtaining it. She thought that, as she only really lived for computers, that it did not matter, ever if she was caught, because she too was intrigued as to what these whalers were getting up to, so she jumped at the excitement that this Sonny offered her. She had heard of him previously of course as he was famous for standing up to the authorities.

What she would do would be to find a low flunkey in computer administration and blame him or her and then sack him, making it look like that he or she was in fact the plant. She would not contact Sonny at this stage as he had stated that the less contact the better. It was vital, if his plans were to be successfully completed that he tried to stay out of the radar. She knew roughly was he was up to, but she would never give the game away come what may, as she too had developed the same sort of mind set about the way the constant surveillance state was going. She loved England and all things English. It was a free country where many refugees were welcome. She did not want to see a police state like other countries where people went missing for commenting on "Capitalist forces." She liked the idea of an American Sonny carrying out an audacious sabotage on the world with its obvious unstated irony.

Adolfo was fuming. What will happen if Draxon Pharmaceuticals found out his incompetence, that he had no report on Sonny attending the Conference. All the money would be stopped and his plans for his own children and the world of fast cars and grand houses would cease. But this was what Sonny had planned. Sonny had wanted to embarrass Adolfo for his role in his incarceration and his phoney look on life. He wanted to make Adolfo look a fool in the eyes of the world's security network.

CHAPTER 3

Sonny had flown into Schipol airport with no worries. And no checks. His plan had worked for the authorities quite clearly had no real idea where he had been or was going. How he was looking forward to Amsterdam, with its liberal sense of atmosphere. He got a taxi to Capitool hotel, a place he knew from his student days when hitchhiking around Europe and although the rooms were modest in contrast to the seemingly hi- tech environment of the Geyser Spring, he found himself back in his element. He sat back in his chair with a bottle of Heinekin thinking of Adolfo. Of how embarrassed he would be. Just like he had been when incarcerated in Colorado State Psychiatric Unit. And boy what an experience and eye opener to the harsh world of medicine that proved to be. Given mind numbing dosages of pills that rendered one a zombie and just because he did not want to engage the research plans of companies like Draxon. Yes, sonny had been a top rated marine biologist but like the famous Jacques Cousteau, he knew that all life had to be ultimately protected. There was whaling earlier in the 19th and twentieth centuries but surely today there was all there was to know. He felt that continued scientific clauses was just a way of pandering to the gullible Japanese public and that more dog food was on its way. He still found it hard that Whales could be turned into glorified dog food. He knew that some die hard greens took all animal welfare seriously, but for him his mission has now commenced. He looked forward to meeting two more faces to join him. They were both due the next day at 2 0 clock in the afternoon.

He left his backpack on the bed and decided to go out and get a newspaper and maybe something to eat. Maybe a snack as he knew the 'mayo com frittes' were brilliant.

He went down in the lift and handed his key in telling the receptionist that he would be out for a couple of hours. He had checked in under a different name. He needed forged documents and what better place to get some than Amsterdam.

He turned left down by the main canal and bought an English paper from a small kiosk. Hotel Capitool was located near the central station not far from the Van Gogh, Rembrandt's and the Rijksmuseum. There was much to see and do in Amsterdam, which is why it was so good a place to hide in as there were scores of tourists every day of the year. He moved towards the Central Station a stone's throw away and bought his 'frittes com mayo'. Sitting at a small table installed next to the ice cream type van that sold the chips he got out the newspaper, the international herald and read about the conference just gone.

The headlines were "Demonstration Again" though he knew different. As he read further it seemed that Adolfo Heinlitz was pleased that there were no eco loonies about to disrupt the gentle tranquillity of both the peaceful and green loving people of Reykjavik. Iceland one of the leading researchers into geothermal energy. Sonny momentarily paused, conjuring an image of the moustachioed Adolfo in his mind, and how he would be glued to his computer looking for people supposedly as bad as him. The he saw an advertisement on another page for Draxon Pharmaceuticals, in which it was stated that they were the leaders into many drugs alleviating many of the world's afflictions." Whilst he was aware for the need top find cures for many of the diseases that plagued mankind a balance had to be drawn up as it was as much about lifestyle as the need to test on animals.

He sat back tasting the chips in the mayo along with his cappuccino. He knew that people wanted to enjoy themselves as that was what life was all about but he had already reached his decision as to how he would mark his time on earth. It was one thing finding cures for diabetes but then it was entirely something else feeding people three Big Macs a day to make them diabetic. He looked all around him on this warm sunny day, seeing the many types of travellers. The Canals, the architecture, the elixir of Amsterdam. He decided to flip through the pages and then saw a headline,

"Psychosadist kills three pets".

He was intrigued and read the article. In Vancouver it seems that there had been an attack on some woman's pet dogs. The police were baffled at the senseless attack looking for a motive. Some green groups said that it just underlined the manner in which modern day man viewed animals as something to be tortured. And there was concern saying that such people should receive harsh sentences. Sonny although deeply bothered by things such as that thought of the mysterious Tanya. She was from Vancouver and had two dogs. Two Red setters. Maybe some form of governmental unit was stirring up trouble who knows, but she would no doubt be reading of this. What would she be thinking. "What a world," Sonny reflected as his face caught the sun.

He finished his cappuccino and decided to leisurely stroll back to his hotel. He could go to the museums first if he wanted or just walk around Dam Square and watch some street entertainers. Of course there was the infamous Red light district which attracted many people but Sonny was strangely detached when it came to sex believing that you were either fated to have a nice girl or not. He had always ploughed himself into his work and when the incarceration had come he seemed to lose track of females completely. But that was not why he was on his mission, though he knew the quack back at his Colorado Unit may think so. All those long discussions with the therapists all trying to understand what made Sonny tick, as if there was some deep, very deep mystery behind life. Sonny was like a lot of people, just fed up with the present make up of politicians who thought that they knew best. Sonny recalled all the computer spin offs from the lunar landing yet could not comprehend how planes still polluted so much or cars, or why cattle were butchered in their numbers for Quarter Pounders', raping half the planet of its trees.

He was not a kill joy. But like the chips he had just had, he knew the difference between an occasional treat and a gluttony in burgers.

Back in his hotel room he felt strangely secure. He closed the curtains from the bright light and turned on the telly. There was a sports channel as well as the host of others including the national geographic, but he wanted to take his mind off things. It seemed there was some basket ball match on. He thought of modern times. Of multi millionaire sportsman. Footballers worth fortunes who dabbled in steroids and the like. Times were strange. He had no quibble with these people. It may have been that in another life he may have played American football, who knows may have become a famous quarter back. Yet he also knew of the infamous Harlem Globetrotters at basket ball team in times when sportsmen (and women) were seen as sportsmen. Curly was a famous Globetrotter he could do things with that basket ball that no other human could achieve. But times were so strange. Sports today seemed watered down and were totally under the control of multi millionaire advertising agencies. Millions went on adverts in the Superbowl, and sardonically he thought for the likes of Draxon Industries. Where were the Curlies and fantastic sportsmen of today that did not need steroids? Sonny pondered and watched the basketball noting its perfunctory performances.

Soon there would be some sort of new world order to shake the world up. He was not worried about what he had planned as he knew he had his beloved Leviathon to guide him through his life.

He watched the remainder of the match also thinking of the great basketball matches between the United States of America and the Old Soviet Union in the Olympics. Classics. But that was how things used to be. The Soviet Union had died out replaced with a Russian Mafiosi and then we had today a world of big Advertising and computers. Everything was revolving around computers. He knew that many would see him as a lonely mad man, even elements within the renowned Greenpeace had not got into the arena of terrorism. But Sonny had studied up on politics when in the Colorado Unit and knew that terrorism paid. It was a feature of governments to appease it by which he meant the likes of Patrick Magee the Brighton Bomber for the Irish Republican Army. He thought it strange that so much money went into fighting the terrorism of Northern Ireland, yet when the government captures someone trying to blow up a load of politicians he not only gets off due to what was called the good Friday agreement, but becomes famous too. For Sonny his message would be that Psychiatry was as much misused in the west as it had in fact been done under the former Soviets. It seemed that many western governments were sectioning people to psychiatric units to alter their views and to deliver their own version of what is best for the people. Sonny had the answer he felt. With the right coercion a new order could be achieved but the actions had to be carried out to precision, had to be done so that the masses could see that they can and should be allowed to think for themselves, free of the huge advertising and pharmaceutical industry. Free of the censorship of vested capitalist interests. He was not a communist. He was not an idealist. Nor did he receive messages from god. At a future date many would come to analyse perhaps his actions. He was, he felt someone who had got a tremendous uplift from knowing about whales in general, and about how they were our last traces almost of evolution on earth. Religious people would probably scorn him, as he saw religion as just another way of manoeuvring the masses. From Catholicism and Protestantism with all the troubles that they caused in the world to modern day Islam, the Middle East, he could in fact see himself as the ultimate terrorist. What had he actually got out of life on this planet. He had nothing save his body and mind. Whereas Leviathon had been around for millions of years. It had to be different to the puny man. It had to be superior to the tiny mind of man. It had to be saved. Also, he knew there would be much name calling such as eco loony, a term propounded by Adolfo, eco terrorist or just communist agitator, but the more he had thought about the more he had become sure that he was right in what he had planned. How he wished that he could swim forever in an ocean of purity, where no filthy remnants of the plastics industry congregated as flotsam, and where there were no oil spills. He was a good swimmer as many Americans were. He had put an advert in some newspapers like Die Bildt of Germany and Le

Monde of France even the Jerusalem post, carefully worded so as not to attract the security services. And the two he was hoping to meet tomorrow in the afternoon had answered. One in German which he had got translated, although the German in question said he could passably speak English, whilst the other respondent was from Israel. He mused at what a pair that would make, though he also knew that he had to remain detached as he needed dedication and expertise above all else. That was what he was hoping to find out tomorrow. For now he would got to bed early and sleep on things, going over the various schemes he had in mind, looking for weaknesses.

He awoke later than planned at 10 0 clock after a heavy and deep sleep. And straight away he thought of the meeting that afternoon. He would need some beer perhaps and food and rang down to reception to make sure some were delivered before 2 0 clock. All he had to do was wait. He was not nervous. He knew that he had a good chance of carrying out his objectives and aims. He was clever and resourceful. What he needed above all else was someone with a good expertise in the ways and mechanics of the military. It was all very well having a high Intelligence Quotient but unless he had knowledge on his side of sophisticated weaponry and other matters connected to that like how ships operated he would be stuck.

The room was prepared with several bottles of beer and some sandwiches. He saw that the staff did not look suspiciously at him which was a bonus. Dead on two 0 clock there was a knock at the door and when Sonny opened it he was met by someone in jogging pants hooded sweat top with a baseball cap. He introduced himself as Ishai and said he was an Israeli national.

Sonny saw the healthy tanned complexion and military look. He knew straight away that this person had been in the Israeli Army. "Please come in," he said in a very friendly manner. My name is Sonny Preston." Have you travelled far. Well, I have been in Amsterdam for a week seeing the sights. It is my first time in the Dam and there is much too do and see. What a City. And the people all speak four languages. The there is the flower trade too. I could live in Holland, it offers a more easy way of life than in Israel, which seems to lurch from one crisis to another.

"Yes, it is sad the way the world works at times. Have you any idea why I want to meet you or placed the advert."

No, but I liked the bit about wanting an expert in adventure. Ishai then went on about the type of life he lived.

"I used to be a mercenary, at one time. I have performed many missions on behalf of Israel. I have served in the Israeli Army up to major and my wife was killed in an unfortunate bomb blast in Tel Aviv. I grew up on a Kibbutz. We all know how many in the world portray Jews as money grabbing pigs, but on my kibbutz there was nobody like that. Kibbutz Amschavin on the Egypt border had little in common with the more richer kibbutzim like Hanita and Amiad in the north. He went on about how he was given orders and carried out orders hoping like many disillusioned Israelis that one day the conflict would come to an end."

Sonny took some time to think then said,

"I need this to be in confidence. The strictest of confidence. I am looking for a special person. If after what I have to say does not equate with your life, or your view on life, then please keep confidence and go about your life as if you have never met me. Can you do that Ishai?"

"Sure. I hope you are not planning to wipe out the jews or anything," he said with a slight trace of humour.

"No, nothing like that. I am looking for a unique individual with good military knowledge. What I have heard so far sounds good. What I have in mind is a series of events, a sort of terrorism but not one that is about human politics in the way that Israel has come about. I used to be an marine biologist but got caught up in a war of research with some companies that I think went way to far in their scenarios, and basically to get to the point I am hoping to strike at the heart of the Japanese whaling Industry to save the whale from being hunted, especially for scientific reasons."

Ishai took time to think also, and then replied

"I like the idea. The whale it hurts nobody. It does not talk of fascism or genocide yet it certainly seems to have few friends on this earth. I will say yes I will help and I can see straight away that you will need specialist knowledge. What have you especially got in mind. I know the last whaling conference was in Iceland a few days ago."

"Yes, I was there. And Iceland amazes me. It prides itself on the one hand of being environmentally conscious and yet when it comes to whales it still followed the line of the Japanese, namely that scientific purposes is the reason. I question these scientific reasons, and actually wonder just what is going on in one of those factory ships"

"I agree."

Sonny continued, "I do not share the view that much more can be gained from research besides why continue to whale. You do not need to research on 500 whales of various species each year. I doubt if there any pristine stocks left such is the bull shit given out by governments."

Ishai nodded all the while. "Yes, I understand you completely. And I agree, nobody knows exactly what is going on which means that something unspeakably corrupt WILL be going on. You know since my wife was blown up and killed I have lost a lot of zest for life but I like your idea. It will test my skills, and maybe give a Jew another name in the world politic besides money grabber. But where do we start?" asked an inquisitive Ishai.

"A good question. You will perhaps be aware yourself coming from an area where there appears to be much unrest of the fact that the many security services in the world monitor groups and people considered to be a danger to peace and the public. With the environmental movement there has been no comparison to groups like the Palestine Liberation movement, if you briefly forgive me mentioning your homeland, the Irish republican Army, the Red Brigades. There is a big list but you also may be aware that the green movement has never engaged in such a brutally, terroristic method. I've studied politics whilst confined in a Psychiatric Institute and it is quite clear that terrorism achieves its aims. Fortunately we are not under the security radar at the moment. It is quite clear that the top experts are more concerned with these Islamicist groups that have sprung up in recent years" Sonny was careful to skirt the issues of Israel. But one goal that I have is certainly to either get inside one of those whaling factory ships or take one out. For me, I have been labelled a schiosociopath, but I am far from mad Ishai. Humans can at times think that they know everything there is to know but inspiration can come from studying these aquatic masters without precision harpooning and turning them into tins of dog meat. You should read up on some of their feats like deep sea diving without side effects, whereas man may develop sophisticated machinery the sheer time that they have been on this planet merits the fact that Whaling should cease. But it does not stop there. My real goal is to strike at the mind set of government that constantly talk of economic growth scenarios and continued rape of the earth, whilst at the same tile starving the green engineering classes of sufficient funds to develop hi tech non polluting systems. A solar powered plane has been developed but it all could have been done much earlier. So I feel the time is right to strike. Set precedent. Of course there will have to be other 'actions'. Maybe the famous horse race the grand national, as the horse too, can be seen as the 'nigger' of the world, and I apologise for using that word, but you get my drift.

What do you think. I mean I know you have expertise, but although you come from a hot bed of unrest, it is an expert that I need. Someone willing to divorce himself from human political mind sets and yet who believes that all is not lost.

"Well, as I have said, I lost motivation in Israeli politics after my wife died. Many Israelis are disillusioned with things. Not all Jews in Israel are right wing fantatics, so it appeals to me. But I am sure at the same time the task, for example of getting on board a whaling ship and taking out the crew and then finding out what is going on will be taxing from a security stance. There are language barriers and the Japanese have some of the best computers in the world. No I like the idea. It is a challenge for me personally. It may get my life back on track. Is there anybody else going to join us?"

"Well I am expecting to meet someone else shortly. And I met this charismatic girl in Iceland by the name of Tanya. She has an English degree and that could prove useful when getting the right message across. What I must stress is that I have never seen myself as a schizosociopath who hates society in general. I know people have to enjoy themselves but with whales being alive for ever it seems, the planet would be lonely without any. Don't you agree. I do not know if whales ever get spotted off the coast of Israel, but I am sure it would cheer the region up. Imagine a Humpback breaching off the coast of Nahariya, to greet the middle East seasonally with its mating calls, instead of all that religious turmoil in the region." Sonny briefly stopped and then cautiously added, "Are you into religion?".

"Somone like me who has had a good training in warfare and with knowledge of what Adolf Hitler did in world war puts up many personal conflicts. I am pragmatic but religion, I fear will always be there, I fear."

Sonny thought for a moment and then put forward a new angle,

"Maybe my other target will be religion itself. When you have been sectioned to Psychiatric medicines it hardened you up to ideas of what is good on this earth. I have a plan to take out The Christ the Redeemer statue in Brazil, target the Shinto religion in Japan and as for Islam, I have fought long and hard as with the bible. Targets. This is why I want people with full unhindered commitment to my 'cause.' People who are not controlled by politicians and big business. People who know that life can be different but still enjoyable.

"Yes, I am in with your plans but the Islamic angle will be tricky. The way religions operate and some would say cynically manipulate, causes the ideas of martyrs. I will not see myself as martyr on this project."

"Of course. I fully am with you there. I do not see myself as a martyr either, though we are likely to be labelled as so such by the many newspapers of the world when they latch on and report our deeds."

"We will see what our next guest will turn out like, but also I feel that a religion is a religion, and these religions cause many problems and have for the mere speck that man has been alive. To know truly where I am coming from, you have to understand my mindset that two thousand years is nothing in comparison to a whale's evolutionary life and biological journey. The sheer time scale numbs me in awe at times. Dinosaurs died out. Do you want to see whales on some virtual reality screen in a virtual museum. Do you want to see animals farmed to the ultimate torturistic experience. A planet where the world of vegetation and animals is gassed." Sony paused again, after saying the word gassed deliberately. More to test Ishais' reaction, and mind set. He wanted to know if Ishai thought him a delusional eco green nutter.

"What you say is convincing. I never really thought of life in that way before. I guess we are a little religobrain- washed at times. But it is audacious what you plan. I feel I have made a good decision to meet you and I am going to help. But it will mainly be on the military side of things. It does not bother me targeting specific religious icons but you realise the repercussions. You will have to get that right and the statements from your cause right too."

"Well, I taught myself swimming when inside this psychiatric unit and I can tell you I fell in love with all things water. Imagine spending every waking hour of you time over millennia in the aquatic phase. The president of Japan has called the whale a mere fish. I fear it is much much more than that. And we are in danger of perhaps never knowing before they are made extinct. I am sure the many children of the world would love to see whales swimming about rather than factory farmed burgerised commodoties."

Ishai then asked the question in disbelief,

"Is that what they are planning to do with them?"

"Yes, the idea of pristine really I feel is gone. And any secrets that whales had into the scheme of evolution may have gone too. The authorities are thinking of factory farming them like cattle farms."

Ishai saw the bottles of Heniken beer with the red star label, and sandwiches.

Mind if I have a sandwich. I have not eaten much recently."

"Yes, I decided on vegetarian but when we get down to work, feel free to do what you feel is required to carry out the aims. I am a realist, but we could input a whole plethora of angles into our plans."

Ishai picked up a white cheese salad sandwich and decided to have a beer to. Israeli culture was not really known to be big on alcohol but he went to the window and looked out over the architecture of Amsterdam.

"You know. I agree with you. People never seem to change. First world war. Second world war. And then umpteen other wars. Gas chambers, suicide bombers, the twin towers bombings, the 7/7 bombings and the many others, and yet the whale swims in the sea causing no aggravation at all and gets its head blasted off. I look out at the fine architecture of Amsterdam knowing all too well what demons lie in the human psyche. I will give my all to this."

As for the Islamic angle it is simple it seems to me, we'll do something to counter that theme. As for the bible well you've got the right target for the Catholic faith. The mafias of this world controlled by the Vatican and the Pope. That leaves the protestant angle, and Germany. What can we of I do there?" At that point Ishai broke off as there was a knock at the door. Sonny said that it would be the next person he wanted to talk to. He opened the door with the card and there was stood a man un army fatigues, beard and longish reddish brown hair.

He said in English with a pronounced foreign accent, that he was called Gustav and that he had to meet someone called 'S'.

"Yes, that's me. Or to be more precise Sonny Preston. Gustav entered with a manic sort of eye stare that was not frightening but just the way he appeared. Ishai looked him up and down.

Sonny said,

"Would you like a beer or a bite to eat."

Gustav in his guttural voice said "I would like a beer and I am strictly vegetarian."

"No problem."

"On by the way, this is Ishai and I also arranged to meet him. I hope you do not mind. We were just discussing the reasons for my placing the advert."

"Ishai. A Jewish name, ya. Please tell me more about what it is you want to tell me, exclaimed Gustav chomping his cheese salad sandwich and then looking for a bottle opener for the Heniken."

"Gustav", said Sony please tell us something about yourself, as I take it you like the animals. Please note neither of us are government agents or the like. I have just been telling Ishai of my plans and it remains to be seen if you want in."

Gustav took a few seconds after a long swig of beer. "I come from southern Germany. Bavaria. I have been labelled by the Authorities as Mad Dog Gustav due to some events where I rescued some caged up snow leopards from some filthy Zoo. But I am basically a good person. There are some in the authorities who have also called me a schizophrenic loner. My family had nothing to do with the Second World War and it was the bit about environmental lover that attracted me from your add."

"Well, I will get straight to the point Gustav. I have an audacious plan to rock various governmental systems of the planet and one part of the plan is to attack those that still whale, more especially the Japanese"

Gustav's eyes seem to light up as he slugged a little more beer. "That is sweet music to my ears. I read about the recent conference and the usual scientific loophole bullshit."

"Yes," continued Sonny "And Ishai here thinks so too. He is from Israel and has extensive military knowledge which undoubtedly we will need."

"Well I have good contacts in the Animal Liberation Front. You've no idea how clever some of those people are."

"One part of my plan I was discussing before you arrived was the taking out or getting on one of those Huge Japanese Whaling Ships. but there are other ideas such as targeting religious groupings as I want to really let this planet's cartels know that whaling is going to stop and that mass animal factory farming of them will never happen.

I talked of the Christ the Redeemer Statue. Possibly an East London Mosque and maybe a Freemason Lodge in Protestant Germany. And then a master stroke of genius to wrap it up either I plan to target the Grand National Horse Race in England. They have religion in Japan, Shinto It is called. But I was thinking of hitting their Emperor. I am sure you are on our side. We do not want to envisage a world with no whales. And as for Snow Leopards there are not many left either."

"Tell me about it. I had the police at Berlin Zoo in total embarrassment when I freed the pair back to their native Tibet. But this idea or plan you put forward it warms my heart. Is it possible though.? As for I speak German and passable English with a little French but as for Japanese."

Gustav was visibly excited but intrigued about Sonny. Then he said inquisitively,

"Where do you come from to get such a fantastic idea from."

Well I used to be a marine biologist at the U.C.L.A. and then got caught up in a Japanese Pharmaceutical research issue concerning Dolphins. I am sure you know all the issues but eventually I was incarcerated in a Psychiatric Institute in Colorado. And I met some types in there. Quite an eye opener and I was labelled a schizosociopath. My reputation was ruined."

Gustav was eager to add,

"The real problem is maintaining a low radar. These are ambitious ideas. The Christ the Redeemer is probably the easiest target, as there is unrest in Brazil and hence a way of hiring people. There are groups like the shining Path and so forth from Peru. I like that angle because South America is where the environment is rapidly being wasted.

"Yeah and there may even be some former Nazi families living over there so we could get a double message over that. Especially as there are new right wing groups coming on stream. And concepts like holocaust denial. I do not know much about Saddam Hussein but the knock on effects are horrific since the downfall of his regime. I do have good contacts in the Israeli Shin Beth but corruption at higher levels pervades many areas of life. But there are still some who try to stop the Nazi menace ever resurfacing."

"Sadly the German Psyche is under scrutiny again" said a wise Gustav, "Yet the guilt in many Germans is palpable. Although Germany takes Green issues seriously, it will always be plagued with the Death Camps."

Sonny could read the complex emotions in both men's faces. "It can be a very sick world at times, which is why we need a very sick message."

They both nodded. And then Sonny knew he had the right two people apt for his plans.

CHAPTER 4

A transmission voice airwave on a radio station playing in Tanya's caravan out in the outer suburbs of Vancouver. She was reading the Vancouver times, and there was a report of some animal hating psychos who had been on a dog killing spree. What a sick world it could be she thought. Fortunately her dogs were safe and lying on some blankets in one of the window frames of the spacious caravan. She now had only to wait for contact with Sonny. She was hoping that there would be some kind of report on the radio about the International Whaling Conference, but until now there had been nothing. Also she wondered what Sonny would think of her in her spacious caravan, one of many on the beautiful park. She came from well off parents but she hoped that Sonny did not see her as just another spoilt child getting involved with the green movement because she was far from that and she was going to prove it once and for all.

The Vancouver Times seemed to be full of the usual spiel about world business and that harsh economic measures would be needed to see mankind into the next century. By now Sonny should have met up with the people he had hoped to choose to carry out this mission, and she was eager to do her thing. She put on a red and yellow bandana and decided to walk the dogs in the clear afternoon air. She was confident that nobody knew of what she had said to the mysterious Sonny and also that in fact not many knew she had even been to the International Whaling Conference. Her two dogs were called Spike and Daisy and they jumped up when she mentioned walkies. She thought that she would amble round the site maybe buy some milk and chat with the security guard. She wanted to make sure her dogs would be safe. It was around midday and the day was clear and bright. She put the dogs on their leads not wanting to upset any other owners but generally speaking her dogs behaved impeccably. She walked through the site staying to the track and saw Mike the security man in his cabin. He waved his hand as did she.

"How's tricks Mike?" said Tanya as Mike stroked the dogs.

"Oh as good as ever. How are you?"

"My usual self. Just after some advice. Have you heard about those sadistic dog killers. Its been on the radio and is in the paper."

"Sure have. I guess you will be concerned".

"I do not know what I would do without my dogs".

"Well, the police have contacted us telling us to be on the guard as they have little idea at present when they will strike next. There were no reports of brutality with people just the animals. I guess you could put your dogs into some kennels for a while whilst it blows over. Probably be some punk strung out on drugs." She thought briefly on what she and Sonny and the gang would hope to be achieving in the next year but did not want to let Mike get wind.

"That's a good idea though I will miss them and they me. But it is better to be safe than full of regrets. It just seems strange why it should happen in Canada now of all places."

Mike raised his cap to get a better look at Tanya resplendent in tight blue jeans and bandana. "As long as it does not escalate and that they capture the culprits sooner than later. No one will rest till they do all over. One minute it is animal rights groups taking on the police, the next a group of animal sadists causing mayhem. It makes my job hard at times. I was once in the police so I know just what carnage drugs can cause".

"Where did this happen exactly.".

"Oh it was a dog competition, I think on the west side of Vancouver. Holy hell has broke out about security. Ever thought of putting your dogs into a competition Tanya", said a bemused Mike trying to change the subject as best he could.

"You know me Mike, I am all Green at heart and I guess I do not really believe in those competitions where special breeding goes on. Those that enter take it too seriously. Maybe some owners got fed up with it all and got carried away with a bit of brutality."

"Thing is they WERE quite brutal which says much about their character. The police are interviewing all the competitors now. It won't be long. Something will turn up. Somebody will talk.".

"Trouble is it is always dumb defenceless animals that get he hurt. Keep me posted Mike and I will look into the kennels". And with that she left to get some milk from the shop, a short distance away.

She tied the dogs up outside on their leads. She knew they would be quiet unlike some dogs that bark continually. And as she bought the milk she saw another paper a local one with the headlines about the animal torturing. It sent the shivers down her spine. Yet at the same time, she dreaded to know what Sonny was planning now with the other members of the gang. But still Sonny had convinced her that what he had planned would be right for the planet and that life does move in mysterious ways. What would all the caravan park think of her if information got out about her supposed escapade with Sonny. And Mike too an ex police officer. She liked Mike and knew that he loved his job, but there were some things in this world just too important to neglect.

She walked back to her Caravan and wondered exactly when she would get world from Sonny. She was very excited. As for her wealthy parents, well she meant to make her mark on the world. And who knows maybe and it was sceptical to say this, maybe her wealthy parents could come up with financial assistance. Still she was not to sure just how her father had made his money. Mafia connections or something. She did not worry. She got back to her caravan and gave the dogs a bowl of water and some biscuits.

Briefly she played with the dogs saying she would look after them from those nasty sadists. The dogs oblivious to what she was saying simply wagged their tails and pined for more biscuits. Then just as Spike was gorging on some great looking biscuit the cell phone rang. She put the biscuits down and got the phone out of the bag, wondering just who it could be and then suddenly she realised it probably would be that intelligent guy she met at Reykjavik. Her heart raised in tempo when she heard his voice at the other end. Straight away he was quick to mention security so he would mention no names. She said that she had been talking to the camp security guard about those sadistic dog attacks, and thought it may be best to put the dogs into some kennels.

"Yes I read about those in an international newspaper in Amsterdam. I do not know just what is going on there. Maybe the pharmaceutical companies were stirring things up".

"Well, how was the meeting?" she asked eagerly. Found what you want?"

"I believe I have, but for the moment we have security issues. I have it off good authority that my mug shot was taken in Iceland. It seems with Iceland being such an environmentally clean place, an irony I know, that my arch nemesis Adolfo Heinlitz was told to make it extra secure employing the world's best governmental agencies. But it was an agent from Draxon Pharmaceuticals that knew I was there. I have some inside sources who can do me favours. And I think that maybe we have been talking long enough. By all accounts we were not connected. There was just a CCTV image of me when the decision not to ban was passes and the scuffling broke out. Adolfo would have loved that. He's labelled me as a total sociopath. Give me your address and I will let you no more of my plans. These cell phone hackers are all over the place."

We can go one better, by using post restante at Vancouver main post office then we can forget about any addresses. Use another name if you like. Well all is not that simple as you need fake identification and although I am working on it takes time. What was your second name by the way?"

"Brown."

"OK I will write to Vancouver main post office soon. Sorry I cannot say more but we must be cautious. Bye. The line went dead. He felt and prayed that no government agency could hack that call. He was a brief as possible but he had to get her in the know as quickly as possible as to what was expected of her. He was in Rio de Janeiro eyeing up one of the most iconic statues in the world, The Christ the Redeemer or Cristo Redentor. He was not smiling but imagining his plans coming to fruition. He would have to contact Gustav and Ishai again and perhaps many times to make his plans come true.

As for now he would enjoy the sightseeing of Rio de Janeiro. He had plenty of thinking to do and planning. He had to get the team together at some point soon to coordinate affaires.

CHAPTER 5

We see Ishai in a Japanese Fishing Port. He had got hold of some information on factory ships and when they docked and all he had to do was get plans of one of the secret ships or get on board for a brief look. He was as curious as to what was going on these giant factory ships used for scientific purposes as Sonny was to blow the Japanese Emperor up. Trouble was he spoke no Japanese, though he guessed an accented Arabic looking for work my do the trick. He could pass as Arabic but why would he be in Japan without arousing suspicion. His immediate thought process was on the size of theses factory ships, which lead one straight away into thinking more was going on than they the Japanese wanted people to find out. If he could get some plans to work on for an attack at sea.

He went on board one asking to see the captain as he was a journalist interested in The Japanese whaling angle attempting to work out just why people were openly hostile to a nations' proud whaling history. After a few minutes some brawny Japanese fisherman were checking him out amazed that he was kosher. Some guy called Ibrahim Illyas looking for a new angle to write on over scientific whaling.

"As you probably know we have problems with whale protestors, but much of our work is scientific," said a man who looked like the Captain.

Ibrahim sensed his chance and asked if he could be shown around.

"I can show you the control room but not around the main bulk of the ship due to research reasons though you could submit permission to the embassy to see if they will allow accompanied tours. Your papers say that you are from Jordan. We do not seem to get many people interested in our work from the middle east," said the Japanese fisherman who could have been the Captain.

"Well, you know how it is. The middle East is a hot bed of wars I am a freelance journalist and am looking for a new angle for newspapers that deal in the middle east. As you know only recently there was an International Whaling Conference Meet out in Iceland. I am looking for any up to date information that will change the current mood and outlook for the reader in the Middle East. I am looking for a scoop on the whaling industry basically. I do not take sides and if you check my credentials you will see that I have never been in trouble with the authorities. I am seeking information on the issue of scientific whaling because I, like so many, do not comprehend the full facts on just what scientific whaling is. I mean do you research on the whales inside your big factory ships, or do you need those big ships to contain all you catch. I know that Japanese people enjoy eating whale meat as a delicacy. As for me I am not here to take sides. I know that there is a bit of a war going on at the moment with various green groups hating the governments of Japan Norway and Iceland."

"Yes these green environmentalists they think we do not manage reasonably whaling stocks. If proper scientific research is put in all can be managed for the good of everybody," said the Japanese fisherman come spokesperson.

"Can I be shown around one of these ships. I am hungry for a half decent quote to sell to the public. Not on the aggressive lines of who is fighting who but on a more green scientific sustainable catch."

"Come up to the ship's cabin and meet the captain. He has only just docked the past couple of days from a long trip round the South Seas. He may give you a quote or two. And maybe a little more on the scientific angle. "Come with me", added the Japanese fisherman. Ibrahim had clearly had clearly got it wrong because this man he had been talking to was not the ship's captain. Maybe someone used to dealing with the public.

Ibrahim was taken aback by the sheer scale of the ship. It was massive. They seemed to be walking upwards for ages before reaching the cabin which had all the hi technology associated with modern shipping.

The Japanese fisherman introduced Ibrahim Illyas to the Captain who was seemed busy debriefing his crew.

"We have had a long 6 month spell in the Southern Oceans and have achieved much research. Our governmental sponsors will be pleased. If it was not for all those green peace nutters out in the Antarctic we would have come back with much much more."

"Captain, this is Ibrahim Illyas from the middle East. He is looking for a couple of quotes on the whaling angle for the middle eastern press."

"Ibrahim Illyas. Japan is quite a way from your part of the world."

"Yes, said Illyas, we seem only to want to fight with one another whilst the forward looking Japanese use the resources of the science world to solve the complex problems that are facing man."

"Yet we need oil like everyone else so science is only part of the answer."

"I am looking for a quote or two. I am not taking sides as I am an objective reporter but It seems with the International Whaling Conference Meeeting recently going off in Iceland it seems a quote won't go amiss and that there is a real market for this kind of reporting."

"We get too much of the violent Greenpeace angle where Ancient hippies drive around the world thinking that Whaling countries carry out unspeakable tortures on our catches. We kill very quickly our quotas and apart from some basic research which some companies sponsor us for we are a well behaved lot. Which is more than I can say for some of those Greenpeacers with their zodiacs in the South Sea. What sort of angle were you looking for. Mr Illyas," said the Captain.

"I was hoping to portray the modern era of whaling with the need for continued scientific research not just in fishing but through out all the fields. I was going to say how this Scientific whaling could find cures for illnesses and ease the burden of mankind whose one big desire to fight wars everywhere infected the world of politics. Ideally I would like a look around your huge ship and then write an article for several middle eastern newspapers. So you do not have much trouble with people in the middle East."

"No. The oil comes from there and we will not be wanting any trouble."

"I was going to lead the article to suggest that Japan was leading the way in the hi tech world and that if it was not for interfering greenpeacers the rest of the world would be catching up to."

"Sounds very amicable. My government will like that. We want no truck with the middle east and all their oil, as we, like other hi technological countries rely on oil too. We need good propaganda. I will just make a few phone calls and then I will be happy to show you around. Have you got all you want"

"I have my camera but I do not know if that is banned of not. I would like some shots of the inside of the ship and then perhaps some good quotes to show the world that it is the greenpeacers who are the violent thugs in all of this."

"Well, my men are very tired we have been on duty for 6 months in all weathers and I can tell you that fighting those maniacs in Greenpeace is hard work. By the way my name is Captain Nyumo Sako. We are one of six factory ships.

Ibrahim was very impressed and from the sheer size of the ships new there was more going on than was being let out. Hopefully he was going to get a look first and see if he could spot anything underhand. Yet there seemed to be an argument going on over the phone. Maybe it was over him and that the government did not want any people poking their noses in.

The Captain came over," I am sorry for keeping you so long. We have to do checks and there are some who do not like meddlers. I do not think you are a meddler and I have told my bosses that your angle of Japanese scientific supremacy will go down well, especially in the middle East. I have been told to show you around. We have got plenty of time. The ships need to be refuelled and cleansed for another trip later in the year. Ibrahim added,

"Well, I guess I need to write some on the sheer size of the ships and how they are necessary to carry out your research and work."

"Yes, said the Captain, I will take you that way first but you can look out from the cabin's windows, and see just how far above the water line we are. We are virtually safe from storms in the southern ocean."

"I bet it is all quite an adventure and I share you view that with proper scientific management all this could be solved."

"That;s good to hear. Come with me. I will allow a couple of pictures below deck. It has mostly been cleaned now anyway." Ishai's excellent memory was taking all the information in as best as he could. The door ways and stairs and although many personnel would have gone there were still many left to stay guard.

"Ibrahim put on his best middle eastern accent and said when they had reached what appeared the bowels of the ship," Was this the place that all the fuss was about and why so many Greenpeacers were so angry."

"Yes, as you can see it is simply where the whales are winched aboard. Greenpeacers think that we carry horrendous experiments aboard these ships and liken them to the famous German atrocities. Of world war Two."

Ishai made a mental note of that. Could I take a picture or two.

"Yes. We do not carry out experiments on live whales or anything like that."

Ibrahim fully believed the Captain. And then he asked the question who is in charge of your work is it the government or does much money come from private companies research."

"I see you are very astute Ibrahim. Yes the government gets involved but there are many private companies who are, let me say, keen to invest."

"A good picture can dispel the so called Auschwitz angle. It seems to me that bad press has partly been your downfall. You being accused of excessive secrecy. Ishai got out his camera, one with a multi memory stick and took lots of pictures. He then remarked to the Captain.

"Seems harmless enough. I do not know what goes on and if you do not want to expound further that is fine by me"

"Japanese people see the whale at just a mere fish, and hence can be eaten like any other food, except we see it as a delicacy. There are no dangers to pristine whaling stocks as we monitor stocks carefully. We take our quotas catch seriously which is all very legal and process them inside these rooms. There is nothing sinister going on like the Greenpeace brigade would like you to think. We have our culture to think about just like other nations do."

So if you like, you simply go out on the Southern Seas and get your quotas and sell the resultant whale meat as food delicacy for your people. So where does all the sponsorship come in, if you do not mind me asking."

"A I see you are persistent, Ibrahim."

"Well, if I am to portray you in a favourable light I need an accurate article on what you do."

"We log types and take samples to see how the oceans pollution effect whaling. Things like that. I know of no live experiments on whales to justify the manic reports of Greenpeace who ram our boats. Accurate data is needed to be recorded so we can see how these species of whales are surviving. | will take you out to the winches." They left the huge room and came across some giant slipways where Ibrahim assumed the whales were brought aboard. He knew it would be hard getting information but he had successfully come this far which was probably further than many other investigators. He was sceptical on the research angle thinking for sure that some live whales were winched aboard to be researched upon. There were companies that were involved.

"Have you any names of companies involved so that I can promote their work." Said Ibrahim.

"The companies are a bit cagey but there is a big one, part of the Draxon Group that seem especially keen to promote sponsorship, but people like me we man the ship. We make up the crew that navigates to the whales. Probably Draxon has its own crew aboard monitoring the science side and taking parts in any experiments. I am paid just to do my job. And it pays well, so I am in no hurry to lose my employment contract. It is a massive job staying out to sea for 6 months or more. Well, I think you got your pictures and you just need some good quotes, if I can think of any. I will take you back up to the cabin. The ship has only just docked the past few days so most of the crew were eager to get to shore to enjoy themselves."

"Are all the ships operated in the same ways. I mean there is no way a company like Draxon could take to the waves itself." Said and by now a very inquisitive Ibrahim, who was getting intrigued by these giant ships.

"I don't see how they could do that with out having their own crews. It seems to me that everything is being stirred up by these Greenpeace Do -Gooders who think that companies are out there researching on every aspect of the whale. The evidence is not there for this. I think sponsors just want to be showing their Japanese patriotism."

"Probably, but other countries do scientific whaling as it is now known."

"Yes," said the captain as he got his breath back from the lob climb up from the bowels of the ship.

"I was going to slant the article with a 'Japanese Science leads the way.' But it is far from easy getting the full information. I am grateful for you allowing me onto the ship Captain Nyumo Sako. I will give you a mention as how hard a work it was crewing these factory ships. Maybe Captain Sako works 6 months flat out to allow the Japanese people to eat their favourite food. Well, I will leave it there then. I will go and work out my article but I will send you a copy too along with some pictures. They were at a port Shimonoseki and the ship was called Nishin Maru and allowed to take 935 Minke Whales and 50 Fin Whales.

"I think with quotas the fleet has got there would be precious little time to conduct experiments. It seems to me that you make these whales into food for your people," said a grovelling Ibrahim.

"Yes there are plenty of whales to go around of that I assure you. The Blue whales and the Humpbacks are banned from whaling anyhow," said the Captain confidently.

"It's been nice meeting you Captain Sako. Maybe we will meet again in the near future."

"Yes, I look forward to reading your article, and to put our side of the story forward. As for a quote maybe 'Japan has no war with the whale.' Ibrahim was escorted off the ship and got a taxi back to his hotel. Maybe he should contact Sonny or perhaps wait for him to contact him first. But as undercover reporter Ibrahim Illyas he had carried out his first achievement. Although it was thought impossible he had got pictures of the inside of the ships and managed to steel some drawing of plans of the ship from the Ship's cabin. Nice work he thought. He felt sure that some type of experiments were going on, and that even if Captain Sako was not in the know, other companies were probably employing mercenary type people to do the dirty work. But just what that work was to be seen. Ishai felt he had done well and that pharmaceutical industries were probably being involved. He was beginning to like his adventure. He was sure that he would be meeting up with Captain Sako again and possibly this would be the ship that they took out in the Southern Oceans. He did not think that he had usurped Sonny in getting a scoop. He how had a plan of the drawings for the interior of one of the factory ships, which would makes things a lot simpler.

But first he would have to write the article to impress the Japanese public. He thought that this would be simple enough. The port of Shimonoseki was on the north-west coast.

Of course with drawings and an actual trip round a ship Ishai knew that it was now more of a possibility to get inside and blow one up if need be. He was not sure of just what Sonny was going to do or have planned but it was to be a finale, or a spectacular to ram home his message that a new world order was needed. At this point he wondered just what Gustav would be doing. He had a plan of either the Grand National in April or the Prix de L'arc de Triomphe in October, and with the statue The Christ the Redeemer in Rio De Janeiro another planned target this operation should be quite an adventure. Targets that were necessary to get the message across of a new world order. He was by now deeply absorbed into this adventure forgetting the death of his wife, though quickly realising that this was a cause to see through to the end.

CHAPTER 6

Gustav had been back in Germany and was lying on his back in bed thinking of the two characters he had met in Amsterdam. This mission was like something from a movie. He constantly played the words of Sonny round in his head. For Gustav, who adored everything animal this was the icing on the cake. He could see the day now when a new world order was called for by governments. No horse racing ever again. No whaling ever again. A world where whales could swim in peace around the oceans free of governmental interference. He knew there would need to be much secrecy and planning. But this dream could be done. Sonny had a presence about him. He was not a messiah with a religious message. He knew that Sonny could deliver. The four characters would one day be famous if not more famous than Osama Bin Laden and other people classed as terrorists who almost brought about world change. Osama had almost ended the pentagon's involvement in supporting the west, but with Sonny this seemed something deeply personal. And both Ishai and Gustav agreed it could be done and that in essence the world's people were sick of the way of things connected to whaling. Of the masses being fed liquid shit from their burger farms and now more than likely whaling farms.

Of course the ambitiousness of the targets was exciting to plan and think about. The Prix d e L'arc de Triomph in France. France's premier horse race. Revenge could be had on the defeat of the Rainbow Warrior, blown up in France, by the French Special Air Service yet what an impact it would have on world racing in general. All those poor horses manipulated and bred for the rich of the world to continue their hegemonious ways. What he must do as an ardent animal lover was see to it that no horses were killed in his 'mission', yet at the same time a statement was made to rock governments into halting the barbaric ways of racing. He felt that he could do the Grand National too in Great Britain, but also felt that you would be lucky to get away with one big assault. It would take much planning as security was bound to be strict. But Gustav felt sure that it could be done. He too would need details of the layout of the Paris Longchamps course. How best to make it happen. He guessed that casualties were casualties. Security must get warnings and so such all the time. What was needed was a get together of the four of them and then their plans put into a workable order. He had not heard from Sonny since Amsterdam and realised the complexity of it all. Yet of all the plans it was the whaling ship that had Gustav foaming at the mouth for action. He could not wait for that, yet this whole operation would need much planning and he and Ishai had not met Tanya yet. So he would need to read up on horse racing in France. He could speak passable French anyhow.

CHAPTER 7

Sonny had made simple notes of the Christ the Redeemer statue, like when it was open to the public but the problem would be detonating it. He had visions of piloting a helicopter at night and firing some missiles at it then taking off in the helicopter amidst the confusion. That would seem easier than rigging the statue up with explosives. There was to be a statement read out loud at the same time to explain the facts to those governments involved in whale wars about how religion was just as bad as any other form of hierarchy. He figured Ishai should get able to get hold of a helicopter with his extensive networks and felt it quite simple really. Timing was really what it was to be all about. But he would have to get the group together for a meet and without any form of surveillance. It would be much harder once their cover was blown. He had numbers for Ishai who would change numbers again once contacted. And the same for Gustav too. Ideally they should find a place where they could meet and talk things through together. He knew that he had been sighted at Reyhavik but as far as his extensive contacts knew that is all it was. Just a sighting. A sighting of a sociopath who had a history of mental illness. He had already got one over on Adolfo because he knew from one of his contacts that he had failed to spot him at the International Whaling Conference. But what of Tanya. Were they recorded together in the hotel? He would need to find out and at the same time find a place where they could all meet in security. He thought of a place in Northern Canada where he could sort of act as an adventurer looking for a team to cross the artic in the name of peace and world co-operation. He would have to put the adverts out to the necessary quarters and organise the meet. But once the authorities got wind of what they were up to it would be very difficult to continue. The Pharmaceutical conglomerate Draxon would be interested to know about him after all it was them who had silenced him when he had refused to follow their research ideas on dolphins. But this was not just about Draxon and one chief executive officer, this was about his now somewhat obsessive desire to stop whaling. He had proven very persuasive so far and had met some formidable characters who would surely help him on his mission, not daft or mad it seemed. And from his perspective it seemed far from mad. It was august 2015, as long as he could keep Adolfo and his team of security experts of his tail he would be winning. Feeling secure that there was no way yet Adolfo had made any progress, other than Sonny just went along to an I.W.C in Iceland he decoded to give both Gustav and Ishai a ring on the numbers that they gave.

He rang Ishai first, telling him he had been to Rio to see the Christ the Redeemer Statue. He went on to outline his plans for this. Ishai said it should prove relatively easy to get a helicopter with the many contacts he had and the Israelis, who still to this day were looking actively for war criminals. He added further that maybe a drone strike would suffice. Many were said to be sheltered in the upper reaches of the Church. It would be no big ordeal doing that just planning an escape route. He said he had contacts that could get a drone in a Brazil and compute it to its target. But if it was carried out at night time they could get away in the darkness and huge city that was Rio De Janeiro. Ishai added that he had done a little research himself working as an undercover journalist in Japan for the middle East and it has come off very well. He managed to get hold of some drawings of the ships that were known as Factory Ships and that he felt it highly likely that some form of research was going along somewhere. But there were at least 6 factory Ships and that some may have their own hired crews by the Pharmaceutical Companies that get involved. That was the impression I got some were above board like the Captain I spoke too, and others were probably infiltrated by private mercenary type crews. But it was concealed well. I have to write an article for the Middle Eastern press under the name of Ibrahim Illyas. Ideallly we all need to meet and get ourselves professionally organised.

Sonny realised that Ishai had jumped the gun on the whaling angle but was pleased he had got some information.

"Well as far as I am aware no one knows of us as a group, although my arch nemesis Adolfo Heinlitz knows that I have been to Reykavik, my plant in his organisation is keeping me up to date with the situation. I do not know if he has cottoned on to me talking to Tanya. I do not know just how efficient their security apparatus is. At the moment I think they did not realise that I was speaking to her but even so it is unlikely they will have put two and two together. The anti whale hunting movement has never produced any die hard terrorists. We have surprise at the moment on our side. He cut off for a while and then continued,

"I was just going to give Gustav a call about the big horse race in Paris. Well, one thing is for sure he is as keen as mustard with what you got planned so you have no problems with loyalty. It seems to me that we have the element of surprise, Yes I need a place where we can all meet up and talk safely. I was going to suggest Israel, then I guess with security being taken extra hard there it would not take long for someone to put the pieces together." Sonny said that he had put some adverts in a paper for some people to cross the artic. And that this would be a good cover and that maybe a meet somewhere in Northern Canada. Ishai felt that it was risky to say a group was planning something as risky as an artic trek as Adolfo would be onto them in no time at all.

"As we are pretty sure that no one is listening in to our calls yet why don't we meet up in London," added Ishai with a perfunctory touch of expertise. Sonny said that he was going to write to Tanya and there was that dog terrorist angle too. Apparently she had been talking to her caravan site security guard about such things. Not that it has anything to do with us. She may put her dogs into some kennels until that blows over.

"Do you think that the dogs have anything to do with her meeting you in Reykavik" said an inquisitive Ishai. It seems so strange why that should happen around now. You know, someone found out you were both talking and wanted to scare you."

Sonny pondered for a couple of moments and then added," Yes, but who would it be. ".

"Maybe some one from one of these pharmaceutical companies wanted to let you know that they spotted you with Tanya. And maybe they put two and two together."

"Yes, you could be right Ishai but why send a message in that way. Do you think our mission has been compromised. It seems a strange way to go about things."

"Not unless you want to instil fear and what better way."

"But that would mean that both of us had been spotted. To be true Ishai I only met her that day and that was by chance, "It seems such a strange and I suppose quite daunting message to leave to the world.

"They know that animals cannot fight back, and there have been no similar attacked in the past two weeks since their first."

Ishai was thinking. He was hoping that they would not be some fringe group with an agenda. I still think that the best course of action would be to find some place in London and all four of us meet up. If we could get more information on these dog attacks it may alleviate our worries over this. And then he added you know this Tanya has she any boy friends at the moment because jealous boyfriends can get nasty."

Sonny reflected a minute knowing what a stunner Tanya was and thinking it rather strange that they should meet up like they did on that International Whaling Conference meet. It would explain a lot, but also it would wreck his ambitions.

"Suppose it was a ex boyfriend it seems one hell of a nasty way to get back at them. I mean strictly speaking we are not boy friend cum girlfriend. I was just looking for people to carry out my plans. People who were willing and she seemed right for the cause. And as for someone knowing what we are doing that seems even stranger but that maybe the case. It could be a lone wolf pharmaceutical company wanting to go its own way.

What worried Ishai was the real brutality of the message. If they were prepared to do that then what else and who was paying them? Sonny said he would find somewhere in London where they could meet up and let the other parties know. He would be writing to Tanya. Then he said to Ishai, please don't think that the only reason I have teemed up with Tanya is due to her looks. I do not think that this group needs a pledge of sexual loyalty. We know what life is all about. And she had some plan of embarrassing the Japanese through their court system. He then wanted to ring Gustav briefly to see what he was doing. Then after a few rings there was the familiar deep voiced German. Unmistakeable. Sonny asked how he was doing, and he replied by saying he had visited the race course in Paris. He said he was not going to harm one horse as for humans well he could not be sure.

"Good," said Sonny. "I aim to get us all together in London soon to better plan things. When is that race in France?"

"October" said Gustav, voice full of nervous energy.

We need to plan our acts as a team and for this I intend to meet up in a hotel in London. Ishai says it s probably the best way forward for now. That's Ok for me, "Who am I to know more than a Jew. This is not The French Resistance but equine resistance."

CHAPTER 8

Sonny had been in London and had located in London w8, a Hotel Kennington. It was situated in an up market area and he would now have to write to Tanya noting that there was no sexual attraction at all. And he was sure that Tanya would want it that way too. He explained his phone calls with Ishai and was now letting them know of this hotel that he had found in west 8 London. They were to meet up on Friday august the 20th and she was to destroy the letter once read and remember all the details. He sent the letter post restante to Vancouver general post office and then rang Ishai and Gustav and left the smallest of messages of where to meet. He still felt no one was tailing them but it perhaps would not be long. What was important was to get some of his so called outrages off the ground before starting in Japan where his real message would lie. A message to the governments of the world.

He dismantled the phone and then threw it away. They would have to make new plans about how to contact one another when they met on the 20th August in a few weeks time. Now he was going to Germany to see or investigate about Masonic Lodges feeling such matters as much to do with the problems of modern society as ever. But lodges could be extremely powerful when they had to be extending their tentacles far into the many hierarchies of the world. He decided that he would get the train to Munich via the euro tunnel and enjoy the ride. Then he would have a look around the many Masonic lodges to decide which one would be a suitable target. He used a different credit card to the one he had been using.

He had plenty of money, siphoning off some accounts via the friends he had high up in America. Not all the top scientists and computer engineers were into the butchery of the whale. He had made some good friends when he was incarcerated although, as you would expect he had had made some profound enemies. Adolfo Heinlitz he knew at this minute would be going through all accounts and records that he could to see why Sonny was in Iceland, or even just to see what he had been up to. Who he had been talking too and where he had been as well as Iceland. Adolfo knew that if he was to be successful with the likes of Draxon Pharmaceuticals he must do his job thoroughly. This Sonny was smart, and it was Draxon Security that had spotted him first in Iceland. Since then he had used everything at his disposal to see who had spoken too and where he was now staying.

Meanwhile Sonny was smiling as he knew that Adolfo was a mason as these members of the freemason lodges referred to themselves as. Yet all the masons were in life for one thing and for one thing only. Themselves. All masons, or the brotherhood, as they were known were pledged to look after one another. Sonny looked forward to knocking the smug faces off one or two freemasons that he had contact with. Yes some were good but basically they represented self effacing greed, and that was achieved by secrecy. The secret society as they were known. There would be nothing secret about them with his plans. He knew there would be a mad witch hunt on when he bombed one of their German headquarters but he was looking forward to the confusion and systems that went into place when they were attacked. There would be many secretive people forced to admit they were freemasons, and the green movement for sure would be in ecstasy with the way society would operate after such an event. After all some said the brothers ran the western world if not the whole world with the triads and the mafia being no different. A secret society is a secret society no matter how you dress it up. And they exist not to look after whales or the top brains in the world. They exist for their own snouts and fed themselves via the troughs that they had placed in every country in the world. But a Masonic Lodge bombing was unheard of and would rock them to

63

the core, which is what he basically wanted. They could do the Arc, the Christ the Redeemer and then the Masonic Lodge all within 6 weeks and then if all went well could concentrate on the Japanese angle. And then they were done. By the time he had finished they should be heroes.

They would need to operate within the confines of South America and Western Europe and then move to Japan. He was hoping there would be no casualties within his team. There should not be. He knew that the list of potential atrocities could go on and on but he had decided upon a few that would ram home the message that he so much wanted. It was the latter stages of his escapade that he especially looked forward too and saw as his master plan. Japan seemed to have got off Scot free with terrorism, a bit like the smug- like America before the nine eleven bombings, where nobody could say it was like Northern Ireland living in the states. Although Sonny was American he was not naïve when it came to the big world of publicity and politics. This was about saving the Whales. Some wars dragged on indefinitely it seemed yet all seem to reach their goals. Not only was Sonny after mass communication but a complete cessation to whaling and he had to get that message across to the people of the world with what he had at his disposal. He was more than happy with the team and could see it working out. He smiled strangely to himself of what a successful plan it would all be if Adolfo got the sack or worse, but the way Adolfo singled Sonny out was eerily strange at times. Here it was a case of use the latest technology which his friends in California had and stay ahead of Adolfo and Draxon Pharmaceuticals. It had to be done. This scheme that he had dreamed up so long ago had to work. To be defeated by him would not go down well. Maybe he should give his contact another call to see what was going on in his camp as it were. This contact, the daughter of a mason, he ironically mused, would be so useful and she was a whiz with computers. He could not see people like this one that he had carefully chosen betray his principles. It seemed that Ishai had already been aboard a Factory Whaling Ship. What resourcefulness, and when it came to the Japanese angle he hoped that he would not behave like a rogue agent. He already guessed that some of the Factory Ships were crewed by mercenary type figures who got money from the big corporations probably of Japan. Hopefully when all this ended he could hit Draxon Pharmaceuticals right in the stomach. Whilst there may be secrets that these monsters of the deep had about research for Sonny the ultimate pragmatist he knew that he would have done his thing for this planet. He knew that he would have got home the message that the whales were not abandoned to be left alone to die by the so called caring governments of the world. That at least would be a direct achievement. To think that they would die out totally without a fight from 'friends' was unthinkable, totally unthinkable.

He would also need to keep in contact with his friends in California as stated, as that was where the sophisticated weapon handling came in. He knew that governments today could spy from out of space and use laser beams to target. And there were drones. A lot to consider on this world. But the world was like that today. It would not be left that way if he had his way. Just to see pristine whales still alive for another million years, although improbable, would be as majestic as their whale songs that had abounded through out the oceans since time began on earth. He had been careful to remain friends with some of the top brains in the world. And although he was praying that there were no traitors he knew that some people would do anything for the right price.

CHAPTER 9

Sonny had written to Tanya and contacted Gustav and Ishai by phone in order to tell them to meet up at this hotel in Kensington, London, a Hotel Kennington. It was not the biggest hotel in the world and figured it would do for their present needs. The Meeting was on August the 20th. As of yet Sonny had not given any of the other members any funds but he knew that he would have to eventually. Hence Tanya used money from her wealthy parents to say she was going sightseeing in London for a couple of weeks to make the trip, whilst it was not known how Gustav and Ishai found current funds.

Gustav said, "maybe Ishai should go and ask a Jewish bank for a loan. Or that brother Ishai should tells us where he was getting his money. Ishai said that he had persuaded his chiefs that he was out of anything military connected to Israel for 6 months. And he was owed substantial money from his time in the army. He was not rich and he doubted very much if the Jewish brothers in the banking world would help him. As he understood things, Sonny could get his hands on any funding that they would need. Gustav said his friends back in Germany helped tide him over. And both of them Ishai and Gustav were stunned by the looks of Tanya in her red bandanna when they met on the 20th August. Sonny got straight down to work,

"I brought you here to London as we are pretty certain that no one has latched on to us. I have took some extra special precautions and nothing has come back saying that the authorities have got word out about a gang of four latter day Whale saviours. He had a contact who could hack into any account and transfer money, either from the government or militarily. But the real purpose of this meeting was not only to introduce Tanya to everyone but to decide what to target in aid of our attempt to save the world from corrupt governments, something that has not been done before. I thought of the Christ the Redeemer Statue at Rio. To strike right at the heart of Brazil and the world's false illusion that it was a green country, with substantial governmental assistance it has not stopped logging. Sonny thought a night strike would be just the thing and it would rock the Catholic church something he felt was necessary. The second target would be the horse race known as the Prix de L'Arc de Triomphe, which he was hoping Gustav would have sufficient ability to pull off.

"I envisage no problems there. Of course security will be tight but where there are crowds they are hiding places. I certainly intend on not hurting any horses. Horses are the niggers of the world. And there will undoubtedly be government ministers or Princes of the Middle East all thinking that they are gods as they bet their money away on their so called prized horses. It should be brilliant."

"The third target would be a freemason lodge in Germany. We all know how freemasons control society, well it would be interesting to see what they do when one of their many halls is flattened. I will be doing this one myself. Should be easy enough. Hopefully these attacks will be in quick succession, as I want to get on to the Japanese angle as soon as possible. There I envisage either killing the Japanese Prime minister or even the emperor of Japan and then gaining entry to a factory Whaling ship to either blow it up or release information as to what is exactly going on these Factory Ships. We could, I know, do more audacious attacks around the globe but we have to be realistic. There will be a huge man hunt. So we need to get planning now for the first stage with plans et cetera and then find some place in Japan where we can base our mission. Tanya, I understand you had some big court case scenario planned in case you got caught in Japan to feed to the world.

"Yes, that's right. If I get captured they will probably put me on a show trial, but I want to use the occasion to explain all the frustration of the anti whale hunting movement. Get it televised and relayed around the world. In fact I think that I should plan it to make sure I get caught but make sure you guys don't. Sonny said he wanted also a spectacular terrorist even in Tokyo where lots of skyscraper windows were machine gunned down from helicopters, to make sure that they would never forget this band of four. He envisaged helicopter flying over Tokyo using a micro- uzi type machine gun to splatter all the glass in memory to all those whales that were caught each year to be researched upon. As for getting caught he had no plans for that. He was sure that Tanya would give a great speech when in court.

Ishai said that any state of the art weaponry he could probably get hold of with his special clearance passes and contacts. Let's have a break for a few sandwiches and then go into detail. Sonny agreed and got room service and asked for a few beers and some vegetarian sandwiches.

Whilst they were waiting for the food and drink they chatted amongst themselves. Tanya saying she had heard much about Gustav's escapades with saving animals from Zoos.

"Yeah, but now it is the big one. The time to save the whale then I will feel very happy. Ishai through instinct looked through one of the windows but saw nothing untoward. But he knew that in time the authorities will latch on, like they always seem to. They had a small team here however and he could not see really where there would be any leaks. There was a knock on the door from room service and the food came. The waitress was stood with a wheeled tray by the door.

"Your food and drink."

"Thanks just wheel it over by the table." Which she did and then left. All innocuous.

Sonny told them to grab what ever sandwich they wanted noting that they were mainly cheese or egg. Then he continued where he left off. We have three basic targets to show the world we mean business. How are we going to go about doing those events.

"We will need weaponry, cash and plans," said an experienced Ishai. As of yet I think it best if I do the Christ the Redeemer with a drone strike, Gustav the Prix de L'arc de Triomphe and you Sonny do the freemason lodge. Then Sonny said he could transfer money into accounts when they were ready, and that he himself Sonny had little real knowledge of carrying out any form of military attack, just what he had read up on the internet. He was not bothered about casualties knowing the time was right in his head for militant green terrorism, after years of being known as pansies. But that was going to end. Ishai said that he could get hold of a helicopter and use air to ground missiles, and use of drones as well, which would make the job far easier. It was getting out after the deed was done that may prove difficult. And then there was the knowledge that after these deeds had been committed exposure of the group was inevitable. He was thinking of some time during September. Sonny then brought up the idea of payment for working for him. Ishai said he was not all that bothered about payment thinking that the cause itself would do him good and stop him moping about his wife's death at the hands of some Palestinian terrorists. As he understood at the end of all this carnage, Sonny was going to issue the world with a statement so maybe some kind of political solution would prevent the need for the group to remain on the run. It is Gustav that needs the street plans probably to cause maximum upheaval.

Sonny said that he could carry out a bombing of a freemason lodge in Germany. Although there were Lodges in most countries Germany always seemed to be in the thick of it when it came to masonry, that would leave Gustav to do the arc around the fourth of October. But what to do for best effect without hurting any horses. The course could have its fences blown up before the race started but how could this be done when there is a race every half hour. The club house could be blown up which would be simpler but with many casualties.

"Still", Gustav reasoned, "if the many race goers wanted to watch the brutality of the horse they would have to pay with their lives. All over the world horses were denigrated into being an animal that was over exploited. A statement would be issued at the time of course.

"Where would we all meet up after the arc." Asked Gustav.

"I was hoping for Japan. We need plans of Tokyo and the emperor's palace as well. With a bit of luck and good timing we can carry out the rest of our plans and bring a halt to whaling. For a while anyhow. As for Tanya I have been thinking. We can include her in a fourth operation before Japan or use her to get plans which we will need. She could of course carry out some kind of operation but I do not know where another atrocity can be perpetrated.

Tanya up to that point had not said much but her presence was very much felt.

"What about something in India," she hastened to add

"I am not sure whether India has ever whaled but there are many large companies that operate out of India. It would be a case of choosing one and then you swatting up on the net on how best to use the weapons. To take out some factory of even its boss would be relatively easy in terms of weapons required, it is getting the weapons in place and then getting out when the deed is done. How do you feel about that Tanya," interjected Sonny.

"Well It would be better if we all did our parts, with four attacks and then to head to Japan. Then we would have fear on our side and the world would know that we meant business. I am sure Ishai can guide me on use of weapons. It is the act itself rather than the maximum carnage from it that really matters. The fact that we are above the law and cannot be captured. The authorities as of this moment do not know of us. We have not got long to get out attacks in place. Gustav is Ok on the weapons front, but Ishai will need time to be able to buy the necessary stocks." Ishai said getting hold of weaponry was relatively simple it was using the weapons correctly that needed guidance. He felt there was little that could go wrong with the Rio angle and with there being a big environmental conference there in the spring, the green message would doubly hit home. Gustav said he had done much reading on weapons like grenades and bombs with time delay mechanisms but Ishai could tell him what weapons were best to use. He was a quick learner. Maybe he could assist Sonny and Gustav at the same time. But Ishai felt there was nothing much to it. Leave a couple of bombs with time delay switches and get out. Security would probably have systems in place to detect such things but they could not cover all angles. Ishai then wondered how his reputation would be when they were eventually found out, as he was the crème de la crème of the military elite, having most knowledge on current and world affaires.

When his wife had died he had lost his love of life that was the Israeli dream, thinking that at times too few soldiers were protecting too many people that were unprepared to fight for their country. He knew there would probably be some kind of outrage that one of Israel's top fighters was involved but he was all for the message that Sonny was going to send the governments of the world whereby the harmless whale had had enough of being butchered in the name of things that were or seemed insignificant. What had the whale done. Surely we were supposed to live on this planet together. And the irony of there being a German namely Gustav and a Jew on this almost divine mission. He wondered what the world leadership would think of their escapade. How would they see the whale then or man's place on the planet when Germany had caused so much imbalance on the world stage.

The more he thought of it the more Sonny liked the idea of some kind of bomb attack in India. Gustav agreed they were nothing but elephant torturers

Why not a pesticide factory. Some of these ancient pesticides did more harm than good for the environment and the Indian government seemed to cut corners everywhere despite their enormous wealth. It should not prove difficult to target the bosses of such factories rather than attack the factory itself and release dangerous chemicals.

"Come let's eat our sandwiches and have a quite drink, there are soft drinks available." Said Sonny to the group. Gustav was not a big drinker and in no way wanted to show off as he could drink when necessary. He had a coke with a couple of cheese and coleslaw sandwiches, happy as a football supporter whose team had just world the world cup in his belief that all was going to plan.

Sonny said," Well we have not got any drawings or plans of any of our targets here. What is the next stage. Do we all meet again or do we do it all by lap top with our individual attacks being planned by each person.

Ishai interrupted, that he felt it better that they planned individually and that he would input the necessary instructions and get hold of the equipment. Obviously the team would have to revisit the targets for a clearer picture. So a lap top with secure codes would be a good thing and would mean they could stay apart until Japan.

"Well," Sonny said, "I want you all to open an account in a false name so that I can transfer ample funds for what you need. I suppose a false name is the way forward although it would take up time and resources falsifying everything.

Gustav said Sonny could funnel some money through the accounts of some friends. This idea he felt was for the world to see this gang of four carry out audacious attacks on what they treasured and then be exposed. They would be detected in time so speed was the issue here. It was august the 20th 2015, and hence they had about 3 months to carry out the four attacks assuming Tanya was going to kill a boss of a company in India. She would need to do some researching there too. They agreed that they had sufficient time and ability to use their own identities. Three months and they would be inside Japan. The finished their sandwiches and looked through the window on a dirty London, where the traffic was busy in the street below. They left no trace of paperwork of anything like that. They all knew by now what was to be expected.

Gustav had a lap top and looked up companies in India that traded in pesticides, and found several. A certain Indiri Patel of Shrai Industries of Mumbai. There are plenty of companies in the big cities of India, I guess it all depends on getting in and out for a kill. Security will be tight on all the executives of those companies.

"What about taking his aeroplane out" said Tanya robustly.

"It would mean more killing but may prove easier in the long run." replied Gustav, "We have to get maps and information as quickly as is possible. How long have we got in this hotel Sonny.

"What worries me is that my arch nemesis Adolfo Heimlich has seen me at Reykjavik and he will be rattling every one of his brain cells to find out why. When he gets a picture of me with Tanya it will get him thinking even more. But even so, she is not that well known amongst green environmental terrorists. But he will be putting together two plus two and maybe he got hold of some of our conversation so we need to plan quickly our individual plans and then transfer all our efforts to Japan with its emperor and their love of whale meat. I just wanted a place where we could freely discuss our plans and then leave it to the individuals with contact numbers given out. We may be not fully experienced but you have to get experience from somewhere."

Tanya interrupted "It would have to be after the Prix de L'arc de Triomphe, but not too long, maybe within two weeks, when I kill the boss of that company. Maybe a hit could be done on his home. I do not know how serious these companies take themselves. I mean green activists know of pesticide abuse but seldom have done anything about it. But whether they have top notch security is another thing. A drive by shooting on the busy streets of Mumbai would be simple to operate, and omit the many deaths of an aeroplane accident. So I guess I need to get some sort of surveillance done. But if your friend Adolfo spots me in Mumbai then for sure questions are going to be asked. I will need to change my appearance from the flamboyant bandanna to more of one of a business leader. My parents have many business interests so I could easily defend myself to having a trip to Mumbai. Sonny said that he would have to check in with an accomplice working within Adolfo's network to see how things were getting along. He got out his state of the art lap top and plugged it in e-mailing some address.

His message was simply <Preston here. What is Adolfo doing regards sightings of me>

They all waited eagerly. The reply came soon after: Adolfo knows of the girl you met in Iceland but not your whereabouts today. He is anxious that something may have slipped by the radar of his efforts to please Draxon Pharmaceuticals. He finds it strange that the two of them should be meeting in Iceland like they did and that they may have a something well passed in the stages of planning.

Sonny said, "dam this Adolfo. He was not the brightest person in the world but he had it in for him. He will have found out that she lives in Vancouver no doubt about that but what can he really know of any plan to take out a whaling ship, the Emperor's family and the Prime Minister of Japan. We must disperse after this meeting and each of us concentrate on his individual strategy and then we should carry out the actions as quickly as possible. It is august now the Prix De L'Arc De Triomphe is not until October fourth. We could by then have the three other projects completed though that will put us right in the spotlight. With just one individual at a time carrying out a task it will limit the authorities abilities to keep track of us. In fact nobody will know who we are a unit till we get to Japan and I am aiming that we will be all set up there by November. Maybe I can use my contact within Adolfo's organisation to feed some false information to delay them. Maybe Sonny is getting married something like that. It should prove interesting or amusing to follow."

"Ok" said Ishai. "We are doing all right up to now but the hard part is to come. We've all got our individual objectives. We should go away now and concentrate on them. We will need methods of contact all the time, because not only do we need to know that the projects have been carried out properly but that we can contact each other to meet up in Japan. I was hoping Sonny could work that out as I am reluctant to get involved in the communications side yet because I do not want them finding out for the time being of an Israeli angle. I will be happy to supply all equipment for the projects and Sonny can transfer the money to our accounts whenever he feels fit. In fact Sonny can begin transferring money now as well will need it for all kinds of things."

"Many people," Gustav teased, "suggested that the Jews were experts on finance but here we had Sonny to outwit the bankers. It seemed he had a contact high up in the finance world of California that could transfer monies but leave accounts looking like they were untouched. But they were, of course, because money would come out of the offended accounts, even though the figures appeared normal.

Gustav continued, "A Jew's dream some would say would be to control all accounts, then a new Nazi master race could not come about again some day but German brains would never allow this.

Jews and Germans did not really hate each other it was these crazed leaders that learned how to control masses of populations." Gustav was looking forward to the day the world's media would label them. It seemed a long way off yet from all this adventure in Japan but they were the right team to make it work.

"Ok everybody come and get your ten million pounds in sterling. There is plenty more to spare but we have to be careful we do not attract the attention of the authorities. Tanya would have to make a new account with a new bank as they were onto her whilst Sonny had many accounts. He could arrange a false identity if need be and this was perhaps one of those occasions. The authorities had no idea of Gustav or Ishai so those two could concentrate on their tasks.

Sonny was in the middle of the room and tried to summarise their plans.

"We have four attacks to coordinate by the end of October. The Prix de L'arc de Triomphe is on the first Sunday in October so if we make that the last of the four hits that means we have two months to work things out. And we need to keep in touch until we get to Japan at least. And keep ahead of the authorities who may well be on our tail by then. I figured that we do the Christ the Redeeemer first, and then my bombing of a freemason Lodge, which I have yet to choose but it could be Munich. Then it would be the Prix de L'arc de Triomphe followed by the Indian industrialist. If we follow that order we should be OK. The authorities will be able to work out that some plot is going on but hopefully we can still say below the radar. Ishai says he can use a helicopter and get away easily in the foothills of Rio. The Indian industrialist may well stick to a rigid timetable which means taking him out maybe simpler than we think. With the Masonic building I don't envisage much security. These people are wrapped up in their own worlds. Which leaves Gustav's race course. Paris is a beautiful city, but we will have the last say over the art of horse racing. Obviously we have no specific dates as of yet. Let's look at the diary and see. But maybe we should keep it secret and let each individual get on with the job, because if we keep e-mailing or telephoning one another the security services and Adolfo will latch on. Let us just say that in two weeks time the Christ the Redeemer will be attacked and each event will be two weeks on after the past, save for the race course which is a fixed time. If we say that we all meet up again one week after the race course debacle we will be going well. And if we release statements to the world that some Muslim terrorist cell is at fault for these outrages we can keep a lower profile. However Ishai may need contacting as he is the expert on weapons. So I have given him a special number. Make sure you memorise it. And don't use your real names if it can be helped. Identify yourselves by an initial, such as G or T." Ishai butted in,

"There will need to be enough explosive for the Freemason Lodge and the racecourse. The Industrialist can be shot at close quarters. We will have to arrange a pick up place. We probably won't be needing much and give me a week to locate it. Timing devices will be needed for the Arc as for the Freemason Lodge thing we may need more substantial explosives."

"There is a master number where I can be reached at all times," said Sonny." Ishai and Gustav you leave separately before us two. At least if our cover is blown it may seem right that there is only one person i.e. me leaving the hotel. My advice is for you to find a place to call your own and plan diligently from there. When all these four tasks are done then we can move forward with the master plan of Japan and a new order. Good luck." The German and the Jew left as of plan and shortly after Sonny and Tanya left, hopefully with no one spotting them. Sonny was wondering when Adolfo would latch onto to his talk with Tanya in Reykjavik. And he would be nosey there too, wanting the exact transcript.

CHAPTER 10

Adolfo was seen in his office on the phone to one of his agents.

"We know he has been in Reykjavik and we know he has been seen chatting to this Tanya Brown a well known layabout in the eco green movement, though hardly a big time terrorist. He had not been seen since though there had been reports that he had turned up in Brazil briefly." Adolfo knew that something was up but what he had no idea." Maybe he has got himself a girlfriend and forgotten all this green environmental bull shit."

"He has not got the resources to do anything." said a cold voice down the line.

"Yes, but he has still got friends in high places, intelligent friends who can do wondrous things with computers. People who can siphon off money and find weapons for terrorism." said Adolfo all knowingly.

"Still, he would not show up at a whale conference on his own anyway. I think he is reminiscing on old times and found love at last. I mean Tanya is a good looker isn't she.? Maybe he is growing up at last. I think we maybe getting as little bit paranoid of this guy because he has a high Intelligence Quotient. Realistically what can he do. Even top Al Qaeda cells got thwarted with all their money and weaponry. Ok we saw him at an international whaling conference meeting in Iceland. But he's has been to these before. He talks to a woman known as Tanya invited her to his hotel room. I mean the guy is flesh and blood."

"What have other agencies come up with" said the voice down the line.

"That's just it. Nobody has reported anything. Like you say there have been so called sightings of Sonny turning up in Brazil but which cannot be clarified. But from Iceland to Brazil that's one hell of a journey."

"There is an Environmentalist Meeting next year in Rio about logging maybe he has got contacts down there."

"It seems these environmentalists always find reasons for meetings. I think they just like playing with the system. That is, keeping the security services busy. They never do anything big like the real terrorists," added Adolfo "but at least we got him on the radar. We are watching his ass and if he steps out of line we will have him. Where was he last.. Apparently he was seen in Germany in Munich of all places but there was no Tanya. He just seemed to be sightseeing. But always on his own. I think he is making up for all that time he was in the loony bin. He was in there for what over three years, it must take it out of you missing out on life like that, especially when he was at the peak of his powers. What I will do is put a permanent watch on his activities. He must have some friends somewhere whom he talks to. Or maybe he is still a bit of a nutter."

The voice down the line adds, "Pity we could not record his conversation with Tanya in Iceland it would sure prove enlightening as to what they were really talking about."

Adolfo then asks "Where is she living nowadays. Still the same place. A caravan park near Vancouver. We could set up monitoring at that end. I understand that the security guard is ex police so that could be helpful. Get on to it, Jack. Get her caravan bugged or something. We don't want red faces when some attack in some city where hundreds are killed comes home to haunt us."

"I will get on to it. It should not prove difficult. Last I heard she had a couple of Red Settters. And she has rich parents that could pull strings if need be for their daughter. But he has not been seen with anyone else. Mind you we have not always been successful in tracking him down, we must take this more seriously.

"You are right" Adolfo finally said. "Right, have to go. Keep me updated"

"Right you are", said a Jack who disconnected.

Adolfo wanted to talk with Draxon Pharmaceuticals to see how things were. Suto Suzuki was the man he often talked to but he knew that they were a big corporation with tentacles everywhere. If he was to get his dream retirement package he must not fowl up. It was a pain in the backside this Sonny affair coming up now. He knew because of his intelligence that anything could be happening. He picked up his phone and dialled a number only he knew. After a few seconds there was a pick up sound on the line

"Suto Suzuki here"

"Hi, its Adolfo. We've been keeping as much surveillance as possible on Sonny and it appears he has been talking to a fellow green renegade Tanya Brown and has been to Brazil. Other than that we see nothing to really report about."

"Brazil, all green roads lead to Brazil nowadays. It seems there is a meeting there next year which will attract all the die hards, maybe he is just surveilling the land. In some ways he had got time to make up too after staying in that nut house for three years. Where was he in Brazil and what was he doing. It seems a million years from Japanese whaling.

"He had been to the university, and was doing the usual sightseeing trips finishing up at the Christ the Redeemer. It takes a lot of manpower and effort tracking these people. We believe that he has recently been in London." Said a confidant Adolfo, who was eager to please Suto because of his retirement plans. "But he has no car and never seems to use a cell phone though sometimes has been seen with a laptop. I wonder what that contains."

"Can we pull him in Adolfo," said Suto "to find out".

"It's not that simple. He has rights after his incarceration and the bleeding heart liberals are on his side. It could give us really bad publicity, which we do not need at this time. But who has not got a lap top today. Everybody has one so it does not necessarily spell bad news."

"I know, but it may lead give us some clue as to why he is going halfway round the world and what his meeting with Tanya was all about. "Look into it"

Adolfo sat up from his slouched care free position and said "Will do."

"Anything else to report," said Suto.

"No, that's about it. When do your factory ships sail again by the way."

"Not until April so we want no bad publicity at all".

"We'll keep especial watch to see if he turns up in your back yard of Japan."

"Okay, that would be good, bye for now."

CHAPTER 11

What ensued since that meeting on August the 20th was to rock the established world. It seemed that three bombings had gone off designed to cause maximum impact on the public. First a Masonic lodge meeting place, the Provincial Lodge Bavaria in Munich, was blasted off the fact of the earth, hitting the vast and powerful organisation often known as the brotherhood. With all its highly placed members holding some of the most important jobs and functions in the world it certainly was imperative that no more such bombings occurred. They had no lead on how it was done or who was behind it. There had been a meeting taking place within one of the rooms at the time of the explosion and there were over 20 fatalities. The police and the authorities were appealing by all media outlets for information and there was a reward of over £100 000 euros for information leading to the group responsible.

The damage inflicted on the freemason movement was incalculable. And then the attack on the iconoclastic statute, Christ the Redeemer. And the authorities were by now convinced that it was some sort of Muslim offshoot planning to destabilise the world and introduce a world caliphate. Government statements were about using every available resource to catch these pernicious people. And that the bombing of the statue had been like an assault on the foundation of civilisation. Bombing these two targets had done its job and caused outrage throughout the world. Ishai too had not been detected as he was several miles away controlling the drone by a computer he had set up in a safe house on the outskirts of Rio. There were many casualties as you would expect but Ishai saw it as just another job, where the longer term goal had more importance. Although he was acutely aware that Jesus was born in Israel, he was also astute enough to note just how much trouble religion had caused the world. He had to remember that this was about the time lord itself, the leviathan of time, the whale. He had agreed to carry out the mission because of what he felt was right about what Sonny said. A new world order in which humans were to respect the earth that they were born upon.

Adolfo mentioned that the character Sonny Preston had been seen in Brazil and that he may have something to do with it, but Suzie Adams the computer whiz kid working for Sonny was doing her bit at suppressing information. She knew that Sonny was now in London and had been seen at the hotel in Kensington on August the 20th, but she successfully deleted that information from the data memory banks of the computer systems that security used. In a meeting with all the heads of security Adolfo said there was no one who now knew where he was so they could not comment on whether he was behind the bombings or not. It seemed very ambitious for a green 'eco-nutter' to carry out such acts. If so he must be getting help, but he was a formidable character. But there were security decisions to make as many Catholics were demonstrating and demanding action, and the awesome power of the freemasons wanted answers too. They knew that they had to tighten up security as many of its buildings were just right for more bombings. All freemason meetings were suspended until further notice. For Sonny the bombings had done the trick so far and stirred up the governments. Sonny thought just how quickly they did their bit to protect the people yet could not even protect a wonderful piece of aquatic biology from going extinct. He would show the world the true meaning of the resurrection. Never again would the mighty whale be butchered as phoney humans worshipped their gods in their secure worlds behind the television.

Ishai and Sonny were holed up in a big house in Acton west London. Ishai was already preparing for when they attacked Japan, Satan itself. For as much as there was mayhem in the world public eye, the Japanese were always regarded as being an insular race. It would take much more than this to stop them whaling but Sonny had the answers. But for the time being he had the world up in arms and the security services going overload with work. And he had a newspaper report to write up about whaling.

Then as if Brazil and Germany were not enough to deal with a leading industrial magnate was murdered whilst coming out of his house in Mumbai, India. A Mr Indiri Patel, head of Shrai Pharmaceuticals. His bodyguard had been shot too and nobody had been caught. Tanya had waited one breakfast time in September for Indiri to emerge from his vast house complex in the Azadpur area. It was relatively simple. There was just a chauffeur driven car by his bodyguard and the road to work. The road was quiet at that time and a simple road block and her dressing up as a police woman to hold the car up was all that was needed. She shot them both as the window was wound down through the head and sped off on a motor cycle used by the police. She was well away when the matter was reported to the Indian state security an hour later. She too was back in London and living now in the house in Acton.

The Indian Authorities merely issue a statement saying that a leading Industrialist had been murdered and was probably a robbery as they were common in India. The statement urged all business men to take extra precautions. Meanwhile the three comrades made themselves at home in Acton. With a big stock of food they could keep out of sight for weeks which is what they would have to do. Three of the targets had been successfully completed. They had just to wait for Gustav on one of the calendar's big racing days, the Pris De L'arc de Triomphe, for the fourth and final hit before Japan.

"Things are going well," Tanya said to the other two." I did not think ever that it would come off so easily."

"Well we have not been caught by the authorities yet, but my source in Adolfo Heinlitz's office say that she is suppressing information on our meeting on August the 20th. Apparently someone reported us. But our source says no names have been mentioned just four people having a meeting." Said Sonny bringing her back down to earth.

"I bet the hotel thought it strange us four having a meeting like that in the middle of the day dressed as we were. On of the staff may have got suspicious. But we will never know for sure. Gustav says he has got it all prepared where to place the explosives and how to get away. He's determined that no horses should die so it will probably be in the main standing area. When the job is complete he will not be coming to join us here, as it is too dangerous, we will meet up with him on Crete, and plan our Japanese adventure from there. We have stirred it up with the world and now the master plan can go into operation. Please do not think me mad. We could hole up here for weeks but best if we get out of the country."

Ishai always the master of caution, said, "security was tight everywhere with the islamicists active everywhere. We can hide for the time being because the world's security is looking for Muslim extremists and that Indian that was killed would be a sign from some new Muslim group. Hindus and Muslim do not seem to mix in India very well."

Sonny thought of Gustav. He was known in animal liberation circles and he had a big job with the race course. It was probably the hardest of the stunts to get away from, and the least popular. The world loved their betting and ruining their one big day would be a sure way to antagonise the various governments of the world. But he had managed to let Gustav know that it would be Crete that they were meeting at after the completion of his mission.

Sure enough. It was the first Sunday in October and the race was big in all the book makers and especially France. They expected record takings and the big race was due off at 4,30 p.m. Then at two 0 clock it was reported that a huge bomb explosion at the race course had meant the event was cancelled and that there had been over 30 deaths and many more casualties. Gustav had shaved his famous beard to avoid facial recognition cameras but had managed to get out of the race course ground before setting the explosives off with his mobile phone which was done with one phone call. It was relatively simple to do, but you needed two phones. The one would be blown to pieces and the other he could throw away. He quickly made it to the metro and got out of Paris within the hour.

The three intrepid fighters looked on at the world news on the BBC news station detailing the carnage. And it looked as if Gustav's dream of not hurting any horses had come true, as there were no reports of injuries to any horses or fatalities. Gustav had placed the explosives in just the right place out of range of the horse racing paddocks. All they had to do now was get to Greece and then think about Japan. Meanwhile Sonny saw to it that various press releases blamed an organisation going under the name "World Caliphate". At the same time he released a statement too, saying that a revolutionary green terrorism unit was behind the killings targeting them for ignoring the environment.

CHAPTER 12

October 10th 2015. An emergency meeting of top ranking security personnel was called and Adolfo Heinlitz was invited. The meeting was headed by Robert Crowe an expert in terrorism.

"I am sure you are all alarmed as much as I am that we catch these killers and terrorists", he began. "They have caused absolute mayhem, with the attack on Christ the Redeemer in Rio de Janeiro Brazil particularly repugnant. Do we have any leads at all yet about who might be behind these attacks"

"Who ever planned these attacks new what they were doing to cause maximum distress and disorder", said a smartly dressed woman called Mary Simmons. She was an expert in religious terrorism with a degree in international relations from the University of California." Nothing," she continued, "was picked up by security about the" World Caliphate", which seems to be an off shoot of more mainstream Muslim groupings in the Middle East. It seems that so much mayhem has been caused in Iraq and Syria that all kinds of groups are vying for control. As for the green terrorism unit nothing was known at all about them. It could be a diversionary tactic. But it figures that there would be attacks on westernised targets like the masons and the catholic church. Security was not tight at the Masonic hall but we have contacted all major freemason targets and beefed up security. Trouble is there are so many things connected to the Freemasons that are readily available to the public. And that attack in India could have been easily orchestrated by the many Muslims over there. As for the Long Champs race course that seems a bit curious in the scheme of things. Adolfo butted in, "Maybe the Animal Liberation Front got involved with this group. We always hear how various groups unite against the common enemy of the western governments."

"I think it unlikely that a Muslim group would work with the animal liberationists, after all their methods of killing animals for food is heavily frowned upon in their circles. It could of course be a diversionary tactic. Of sorts. But terrorism is terrorism. These groups whomever they are need finance.

Adolfo again chipped in." We have a character called Sonny Preston under the radar, though his exact whereabouts at this moment are not known. He is a very resourceful and intelligent man with a chip against the world. He has been reported as being seen in Iceland after one of those International Whaling Conferences but strangely he has also been seen in Brazil."

"What is his cause?" asked Mary

"He was held in a state psychiatric facility in Colorado for three years for coming into conflict with Pharmaceutical research on dolphins, but he has contacts and is highly intelligent. Apparently he was seen talking to this girl in Reykjavik. Pictures of both people were displayed on the screen.

"Look a real pair of drop outs" joked one official sat around the table. "What do we know about the girl?"

Adolfo again took over the meeting saying she was Canadian with interests in animal salvation and that her parents were rich. But it might have been a chance meeting as we have heard absolutely nothing from our field operators about these two. But I have a feeling about this one. The psychiatrists reports about Sonny said that at times he was on some kind of mission to end Dolphin research. He may have been planning this ever since his release.

Someone interrupted saying, "Most Dolphin research is in Japan so why has he not struck there if it is him." Mary intervened "Maybe he has plans to do just that, but it seems to me to be beyond the scope of these two to finance this sort of thing. I like the Muslim angle better, it fits with three of the targets.

Why can not we get any information on present whereabouts of these two people. Adolfo said," we were just doing routine security checks of people at the International Whaling Conferences, which was before any of these terrorist events happened. It seems there is no trace of them after these events." Robert Crowe intervened.

"It seems that we have got little about little. We must do better than this. We have some of the best computer security equipment in the world."

"Did have", said a small voice from a Raymond Homes." A lot of our state of the art was infected with a virus after the Race course attack. It must be them. And it would take some doing he must have inside help on this. I don't know if we have any sympathisers with the animal liberation cause but Muslims appear to be able to infiltrate many of our systems, and we hear of many people ready to convert to the ways of Islam."

A furious Robert Crowe shouted,

"Are you saying we have nothing to go on whatsoever other than a sighting in Reykjavik, which was probably a lovers' meeting if the truth be known. He must have had a terrible time in that Psychiatric facility and then after all the years found himself a girlfriend. We do not know if they are involved or not as we do not even know where they are?"

Adolfo said, "If the Muslims have some new computer genius then it will prove difficult."

"I have every major Catholic, Mason and governmental figure wanting results but we have none. I don't know whether to release the pictures of the two or not. You know what it is like you get the wrong people and then get your ass sued for misuse of public money. I will have to prepare a press release of some description to alleviate public worry. And the bookies are getting at me asking for increased security. But let's look at the facts.

We have a leading Masonic building in Germany blown up. It would not take much to carry this out. Second we have the blowing up of the Christ the Redeemer Statue. It seems the genius behind this used a drone. Usually drones are only available to western governments which leads me into thinking that some kind of military brain is at work here. A specialist with vast knowledge of weaponry. Third the killing in India may not have anything to do with these other bombings but the Indian business community are up in arms demanding an increase in security. Again it would have been relatively simple to do this. There were reports of a female police officer on a police bike at the scene but we have no photographs. Fourth, the race course. This would have been harder due to the security and it seems as due to the fact that no horses were harmed that it was an animal lover."

"So as you can deduce yourselves we have mixed messages here. I know a statement was released in which it was stated that the "World Caliophate" was responsible, but this could have been a clever decoy."

Mary Simmons intervened again. "There must be scores of animal lovers and groups out there that would like to do something like this. I be that if we look close enough several names would crop up who would want to carry out such an act. We have two groups claiming responsibility the World Caliphate and a green terrorist movement. But nothing much to go on.

Robert Crowe said quite sombrely,

"We must make sure there are no more attacks, which is going to test out services to the limit. Chances are these people are lying low somewhere until the heat is off. But they will need identification, bank cards et cetera to get by. We can only hope that they turn up sooner than later even if it's just for elimination purposes.

CHAPTER 13

The four of them, Sonny, Gustav, Ishai and Tanya were staying in a house on the outskirts of Heraklion Crete.

"So what's next", asked Tanya. Just about every cop in the world will be on the alert and looking for us."

Sonny replied. "Well, my guess is that there will have been a top meeting of senior security chiefs and that some if not all of our names may have come up. Me, I am well known and one security official in particular, an Adolfo Heinlitz is obsessed with me. But let us take stock. We have carried out our tasks and are causing havoc on the world. Chances are they suspect Muslim militias, which seem to get bolder day by day. Gustav has shaved his beard off and cut his hair so he looks now nothing like the many photos they will have of him on file. Ishai probably remains below the radar, yet they could be on the look out for Tanya with her rich parents as she was seen with me in Iceland. What we've got to do is get into Japan and complete the second part of our work and my contact at Adolfo's head quarters can only cover for us for a while. Adolfo is sure going to latch onto me sooner or later as long as we can get into Japan before arousing any attention.

I have friends in America who let us use this house, and I should think we are relatively safe here for a few weeks if we keep a low profile. But the quicker we get out selves sorted out for the Japanese strike the better. We've got the Emperor to kill, and we got the blitz on the centre of Tokyo and then the finale with the whaling ship. Ishai said that Japan was new to his way of thinking with the Israelis concentrating on war criminals in South America. They would need equipment over there to cause the blitz on the skyline of Tokyo.

Sonny said they had got a safe house on the west coast of Japan, it was getting there now that the heat was on. They could go one at a time as four in a group may arouse suspicion, and there were passports and other identification needs to be sorted out. By now Sonny had grown a beard something he had not done for a while. It would help him from being identified. His source Suzie Adams in Adolfo's security team said it was only a matter of time before pictures were released of the four of them in London. Sonny realised that to get to Japan they would have to act fast. His friends from the University of California had used their substantial expertise to manufacture fake passports and credit cards. He decided that they should go soon so showed the new identities to his comrades and told them the address of the safe house in Kanazawa on the west coast of Japan. That is where they were to meet up. They had a computer in the room and looked up ways of getting to Japan. If need be one could go by boat. Sonny had said that the hunting of the whales often did not start until April. So as that was to be the last act in their' reign of terror' they had more than enough time to plan the assault on the Factory Whaling ship. Get inside and go with it then attack. It seemed the best thing to do.

Tanya was using the computer and noticed that you could fly from India to Tokyo and asked the rest of the gang if they thought it was wise for her to do that having killed the pharmaceutical magnate.

Sonny replied that as of yet they were unknown. They probably had a few days left before their names were made public. That is why it was imperative they get to Japan within the next few days. Yes it was risky to go back to India but if it meant it was quicker getting to Japan then he felt it okay. He himself was going to fly to Moscow then get a flight from there. Ishai said he was going back to the States first then getting a connecting flight. Gustav did not want to go back to Germany as he was well known there beard or no beard so he thought he would get a flight from Istanbul direct to Tokyo. Tanya decided after all to go via Pakistan. They were plenty of flights available. They went through the new passports and credit cards and began to tune in to the next half of the mission, where hopefully the world's many governments would take the group so serious that they would call a halt to International whaling.

They had been lucky so far with all going to plan. Four audacious terror attacks designed to whip up the media and the public to fever pitch about the 'World Caliphate', whilst they slipped beneath the radar to the real goal of Japan. Ishai said he had got the arms sorted out and was tapping away on the computer to one of his sources in Thailand to arrange a few minor details.

What was worrying him was when decimating the skyline of glass of Tokyo, which would need a helicopter was getting away afterwards as the government would call in the army and they could be quickly over run. Getting hold of a helicopter whilst relatively easy for a man of Ishai's contacts was problematic too. But he had located an old airfield outside Tokyo where it would be delivered. His contacts did not question Ishai for they knew what an awesome soldier he was, Anything he had ordered must be in good faith. When Ishai had finished with the computer he told Sonny it was all set up with arms delivered to the safe house.

"Good" said Sonny. "Let's get some sleep and we will be away tomorrow. We do not need much luggage but some is a necessity to prevent suspicion. Get your stories straight as to why you are going to Japan if you are questioned. Hopefully we will all sail through customs. It is then likely that Adolfo's security apparatus will have pictures of us and we won't be popular with the public until we have done our thing in Japan. I envisage a public liking of our escapade in Japan although as for Catholics I am not so certain they will forgive us, but if that is what it takes to wake the world up from its glorious religious systems and beliefs so be it. Gustav looked at Sonny whilst brimming with pride. If Gustav survived this ordeal in Japan he would be a true hero to the animal liberationists in Germany of which there were many. No doubt the police were questioning these groups. They all hit the sack and eagerly awaited the morning to go one by one out of the house in Heraklion, Crete and make their way to Japan individually. They knew that they had only a few days to play with.

It all went to plan next morning. They were all up by 5:00 a.m. and did some packing and rechecked their schedules with the various airports. Their false identities were convincing. And off they went leaving Sonny to go last who had a contact to clean up after them. They were not nervous as they saw themselves on a mission to save the true inheritor of the planet from its extinction. Which would surely happen if someone did not try and save it. Already some species of whale had become extinct. The four of them knew that there was no other way. That whaling would never stop without some kind of military input. They did not really care for casualties as they saw the whale as something that must be protected at all costs. Sonny was pleased that he had found three other people who thought like him. Especially pleased that he had found the Israeli Ishai who was adept at his work. One felt safe with him on your side. He had lost his wife in the conflict of the Middle East but saw the whale as something that over passed the whole of humanity. The sheer scale of time that they had been around meant the planet would be lonely once they died out. And with their message at the end of the operations going out directly to the world, maybe some wars would stop too. Time was too precious a thing to neglect in the scheme of creation. Sonny felt happy that after his years of incarceration in a psychiatric institution he was now finally getting his own say, that creatures other than man had a right to roam the planet safe from big business and corrupt governments. With Gustav he had someone who lived for animals and their welfare and Tanya was as dedicated to the cause as any religious worshipper.

PART TWO

PART TWO

CHAPTER 14

It was three days later October 25th that the band of four eco warriors found themselves reunited at the safe house in Kanazawa near the Omicho market. There was a lot to see in terms of the art world in Kanazawa but that would have to be put on hold.

Their stay in the safe house attracted little attention from the rest of the market area. Sonny asked how their flight had gone and they all said surprisingly well seeming as they were big time 'terrorists' in the eyes of the world. Tanya said she was pestered by some men for her looks, but it was nothing she could not shake off. She must make herself look more plain and stop wearing her trade mark bandanas.

"Well listen up everybody. The next bit of action is particularly risky. Killing the emperor of Japan, maybe in his palace. As I intend taking out the whaling ship in the spring when they set sail, we have plenty of time as it is only the end of October now. I have a map of the area around his palace. On December 23 and January 2 thousands of well wishers file across the Nijubashi to greet the Royal Family, although they are lined up through bullet proof glass. Apart from these two days, the general public is only admitted to the palace grounds on pre-arranged official tours, conducted in Japanese but with English Language brochures and audio guides available. It would be one thing to take out the emperor in his own palace, yet we do not know fully his list of engagements so we could target him out of the way of bullet proof glass. If we knew specific engagements where he may open events or turn up at a baseball or football match, things would be much easier, but emperor Hoto is quite a reclusive figure. In order to hit the Japanese psyche his death is a must and if we can get the Japanese prime minister so much the better. This country leads the way with modern day whaling paying no respect to negotiated treaties by the International Whaling Conferences. So we have to strike hard and be decisive. It is audacious, to say the least but we have enough time to plan. My friends in California have made sure that money is no object with their ability to interfere with banking computers. I will get hold of a list of engagements from the tourist office. That should be easy enough and we will see if there are any engagements where he can be taken out other than his bullet proof palace."

Tanya interrupted. "We have got time so far, but Adolfo will no doubt know of us and the world will have our pictures in the press and on television."

"Yes, we are under pressure to get this done before our identities come out. I have addresses where we can hang out for a long time if need be but ideally we need the Emperor to go outside to an engagement where say Ishai can target him with a sniper's rifle. I don't know whether he is a baseball fan or not because the Tokyo Dome would be an ideal place to do a hit from one of the hospitality boxes or directors boxes as they are better known as. He must get out sometime. He cannot hide away behind bullet proof glass in his palace all of the time. Or it may transpire that we can get into the palace. But we must think fast and organise our hit. When we've done that we can cause havoc with the skyscraper skyline of Tokyo and maybe kill the prime minister and then go into hiding before the attack on the whaling ship. There are always visits to various shrines, some to honour the war dead, There is one such visit on November 15. Chances are the Emperor will be there but I will need to confirm it with the tourist board. And although he will have strong security a well placed sniper should be able to shoot him."

Ishai told them that he had access to state of the art sniper rifles that can shoot through glass first and still hit the target, and with infra red sights it was just a question of getting a good shot at him out from behind his bullet proof glass palace.

"Good" said Sonny, full of delight as someone knowing that the prize was within sight. "I'll go and find a list of his engagements and then we will discuss it further. What about you Ishai can you get your sniper's rifle within the next few days."

"I have been onto an old officer friend of mine in Israel, telling him some story about hunting neo Nazis and that one or two may need taking out, so they trusted my judgement and allowed me the sniper's rifle. As for the taking out of the skyscrapers we will need a helicopter with micro -uzis to strafe all the glass, along with the government buildings. So far my friends in Israel believe that I am still grieving the death of my wife and that as a consequence I am allowed time out of the Israeli army's affaires. However, the fight was not just against militant Palestinians. They were, the world over, thousands of die hard neo Nazis determined to bring about the destruction of Israel. His comrades in Israel gave him virtual carte blanche to take out threats. There were Nazis in Japan who hated Israel just as much as many Palestinians.

"Right" said Sonny I'll just nip out to the local tourist office. You three can get some rest or continue planning. Remember we have to take out that whaling ship in the spring. That will be the best target of the lot as far as I am concerned. If we are successful and as of yet I see no reason not to be, we will halt all whaling on earth and once more the time lord of the seas will be free to swim around the earth's waters. I find it hard that some whales still swim the oceans as there is that much junk in the seas. But we can only do our thing. Some species of whale are already extinct. Let us not inherit a world where there are none."

Gustav said "We will not let you down. We have caused mayhem already. The world, according to the news on television has gone apoplectic with our attacks so far especially on the stature of Christ the Redeemer. Catholics, of which there are millions, feel there whole way of life is under threat. For once religion will have to stand up and take responsibility for other creatures besides that of man. I have always felt the church to be full of bullshit, I mean just look at how rich the Catholic church is. What we fight for is far more of a cause than the belief that the son of God pays for our sins. It is still mainstream news our attacks but some of the heat has died down. But it seems that we may have been grassed up from that meeting in London. Well, we can change our facial features, but if they are looking for four of us it will make it relatively easy for the authorities. Maybe we should split up until we find when this Emperor has any visits to make. Personally, I think being in Kanazawa means we have got more time. We may have to carry out both attacks in Tokyo in relatively quick succession just to get things done. Once news gets out about the emperor the people will be up in arms. But that is when we can strike right away again, crushing the glass skyscrapers and hopefully the prime minister of Japan. So supposing he does venture out on November 15, why cannot we carry out both attacks the same day. It is worth thinking about."

"Yes, I agree," said Sonny happy to see all of his team were geared up for the forthcoming bonanza.

Tanya said" Can we get a helicopter by then, and if so who is going to have all the fun with the micro- Uzis."

Sonny simply answered that he thought it best if Ishai piloted the helicopter and Gustav did all the shooting. If they were both to get the Japanese Prime minister they would have to strafe the entire government building complex and know beforehand where the prime minister would be. That was something else to find out. It could be that he would be at the shrine too, saying prayers to the dead of world war 2. That would make things easier."

Tanya added, "What a coup that would be. Two birds with one stone. But it puts a lot of strain on Ishai using the sniper rifle and then taking a helicopter up over the centre of Tokyo, and then there is the escape as the resulting mayhem will rally all of the governments defensive forces."

"I have full faith in Ishai," said a beaming Gustav. He will find a way out. Maybe if we carry out the attack at night time it will make things more difficult. I am just counting on Ishai getting the best helicopter available."

Ishai said," I can use my military influence again by saying I need one to track these neo Nazis to their hide ways and to get about Japan. But there is much planning to do yet. We are not sure that the emperor will visit this shrine on the 15th but the chances are he will. We have about two weeks to plan it all.

"Well," said Sonny," I am on to that right now. I will see you all later for when we eat."

Sonny was in two minds whether to contact the tourist bureau in person or give them a ring. He knew phones could be tapped and then again staff may remember his face. Eventually he decided to visit the local tourist off ice of information and said that he was a visitor from the states staying with some friends and was interested in seeing the Emperor and that he understood that there maybe a visit to a shrine on the 15th November. The clerk in the tourist office checked her computer and after a brief pause said that was the case and that the prime minister of Japan would be there to accompany him. It was an annual pilgrimage. The clerk then printed off some information in English and gave it to him.

He exited the building then spotted a newspaper kiosk and saw a headline on the International Herald,

'No new leads on the terrorist outrages'.

Sonny thought that good but did not buy the newspaper. He could get an update when back at the house. He did not want to be recognised, and adjusted his sun glasses slightly. He felt quaintly amused that the best of the world's security services could not track them down. Surprise has always been the best form of attack. He noticed the streets were busy with people and cars. He thought of going for a coffee or a snack in the many places that lined the main street, but then did not want to attract attention to himself, as foreigners tend to stand out from the non multi-cultural Japanese. The festival on November the 15th was called Shichi-go-san. It said in the tourist literature that normally it was a children's festival but this year the Emperor and the prime minister would be attending in the centre of Tokyo. They would need detailed maps of the area so that Ishai could find an adequate place to fire his state of the art sniper rifle. Yes there would be children in attendance but this was their best line of attack. He went back to the safe house and told the others the news. He told them that the Emperor and the prime minister were both celebrating the festival of Shichi-go-san on the 15th November. Whilst this was not normal it was felt that they should do their bit with the children. Ishai said that we needed to get to Tokyo soon and plan the shoot and then there was the helicopter with the micro-Uzis to set up. It was a lot to plan in a few days but Sonny had found them a secure flat near the wholesale market in central Tokyo. The busy market should give them some cover from the security services.

But for now it was meal time and then back to work after the meal.

I

CHAPTER 15

Another security conference was in session in which Adolfo reported that Sonny was indeed part of that four seen in the hotel in Kensington but since then they had disappeared off the radar. Robert Crowe, the expert in terrorism asked about facial recognition technology to which Adolfo replied,

"It seems most of the facial recognition technology was hacked into by persons unknown a little after they left that hotel in Kensington west London. They must have influential and people with high expertise on their side because we've come across nothing which should have been a cinch had the technology been working. It has only just been restored but you can bet it has been interfered with to blot out all traces of their movements."

"God knows," blasted Crowe, "We must have some of the best personnel alive and we have been out manoeuvred. What's the current status?"

"Well", said a nervous Adolfo," we have had reports of sightings all over the world many of which we are checking out but so far they are eluding all our attempts to track them down. But when you think of what their hackers are capable of they could be sending false reports and false pictures. But one thing we are sure of Sonny was in that four and that he has got friends in the right places. A lot of top academics and military people sided with him over the way he was treated, as it was obvious that people who did not tow the line could end up in psychiatric detention units. It seems what ever he has been planning he has been planning for a long time, though just what he is after we do not know. If that gang of four was responsible for those terrorist events of October, then he must have a reason. Either he has been planning his revenge or he is on a mission about something. As for those god dam psychiatrists that let him out early they have a lot to answer for." At this point Mary Simmons interrupted.

"Are you sure that these outrages are them. It seems a bit drastic for revenge to do what he did. I still like the religious angle, as Muslims are by now experts at hacking and utilising western computer systems. It could be that these four were merely celebrating Sonny having found a new girlfriend, what's her name." She checks her records. "Tanya Brown daughter of a very rich family. It seems she lives on a caravan park on the outskirts of Vancouver with her two Red Setters, far from committing terrorist outrages around the globe."

"Where is she now?"

"We've no idea. We have had reports from security at the Caravan Park that the last they heard from her was when she was inquiring about putting her beloved dogs in kennels due to those dog killings in Canada. And that was weird too."

"Yes I recall those sadistic killings", said Crowe. "Well what should we do now. Maybe we should print the picture of the four from that hotel in Kensington in the world's press. Even though they have likely altered their images it is surprising at just how observant Joe Public can be when hunting down people. But I don't like it. If it was a Muslim terrorist outrage they would be likely be planning something extra to ram home their perverted message of Islam. And it if was a Muslim angle, we have no leads whatsoever."

Mary Simmons agreed that a picture of the four would reap dividends in terms of coverage in the media. "We may well have to rely on public sightings."

But little did they know that Sonny had more tricks up his sleeve. He had already successfully used his resources to blame the organisation World Caliphate, now he was going to use his friends knowledge to put more disinformation out to the media with pictures of people behind the outrages. He figured that if he made out some security organisation had found the terrorists in say Pakistan, it would take all the heat from his gang. So the next day, the first of November 2015, all the papers of the world were printing that the Muslims behind the outrages had been found in Pakistan and that they would be brought to justice.

Hence another security meeting and Robert Crowe was up in arms.

"Which security group came across the pictures of these Muslims and why wasn't I told when it happened."

Adolfo seemed apologetic and said it all happened so quickly. Apparently a security organisational hi- tech team from Saudi Arabia had located the group calling themselves 'The World Caliphate'. The team in Saudi was a specialist organisation set up by the ruling Princes to tackle the rise of religious extremism and more importantly to stop it collapsing stable regimes of the Middle East.

"Well it will have to be examined thoroughly. It could be another genius trick to divert attention. What do you think Mary?

"The Saudis have become increasingly involved in security fearing the collapse of its own government from some of the many terrorist groups out there. They have put a lot of money and resources into combating terrorist infiltration into their country. From all accounts, this 'World Caliphate' was hiding in a remote village in Pakistan when they were rumbled. Their leader it turns out is Whalid Sadique and he leads a band of mercenaries prepared to do anything it takes."

But as of yet, Mary Simmons did not know that it was all part of an elaborate plot to hide the real terrorists from the public eye. And subsequently, all the press were showing pictures of this small village in Pakistan along with Whalid Sadique, who had agreed to go along with the whole experience. It would be some days before the security services would latch on to the fact that they were bogus.

Back in Japan Sonny and his three friends were listening to all the news releases on the many news stations they could obtain in English. And the heat was off. They could now concentrate on shooting the Emperor, and the Prime Minister in a few days relatively secure that they had not been detected. But after the shootings things would be tougher. He knew that in his heart he was right to kill the Japanese Prime Minister as that person could end whaling from his country tomorrow but always took sides with the whalers.

Now was the time to hire a car and drive to Tokyo to their place of safe hiding. Ishai too, had the sniper rifle to pick up from a contact and the helicopter to sort out after the shooting to enable them to decimate the skyline of Tokyo. The car they hired was a Nissan which would melt into the background of any car park. It was November 10th and they made their way to Tokyo from Kanazawa on the left hand side of the road with Gustav Driving. They left Tanya behind in the safe house to help plan the mastermind raid on the Whaling Factory ship. They were heading for the wholesale market area in central Tokyo. They would need time to set up the sniper hit on the fifteenth of November.

The drive went really well with no problems. Gustav had driven cars on both sides of the road in his time so this was no problem. It proved hard though finding the exact spot of the flat or safe house in the wholesale area, with various maps being used and eventually they found themselves parked opposite an old building with various Japanese signs stuck on the walls. Neither of the three had any idea what the words meant but they found the apartment eventually and let themselves in. They were wary at first thinking they many have been found out but slowly they adjusted to the darkish light and looked through the windows at the busy market where there were meat and ironically fish being sold. Sonny wondered if there was any whale meat being sold today. Chances are there was.

"Murdering bastards" he thought and Gustav read his mind too. Ishai, the cool person that he was brought them back down to earth,

"We've got four and a half days to organise this hit and then stay undetected as we get the helicopter airborne to carry out the blitz. We need micro -Uzis for that to strafe all the glass in the skyscrapers. If they did not know of us before that they will after. We have to get that done and then get away which I have been thinking about. I have been studying the area of Tokyo and there is a park or garden that I can land on after the damage has been done. We won't have long but if Sonny meets the pair of us by the entrance to the garden which I think is called Meiji-jingu inner garden, we should be able to get away in time. Sonny will have to prove himself a good driver.

CHAPTER 16

It is the 13th of November. Ishai had been into town on his own dressed casually to get hold of the sophisticated sniper rifle from a military contact who asked few questions only that it was great to see Ishai again after so long a time. Isahi reminisced with his friend Zelig about old times and Zelig said he was hurt to have learned about his wife. He did not ask about why he needed the sophisticated sniper rifle, feeling that there must be a good reason. The rifle was surprisingly compact and easy to carry in its fold away case. All he had to do now was find a good spot across from the shrine to hit the two v.i.p.'s. He was rewarded as there was a high rise building a few blocks away allowing his space to look down on the target shrine. He found an old dirty room with a window looking back towards the shrine and got out his sniper rifle. It was light weight and had mega scopic sights making long range objects appear near. He assembled it as he remembered and looked through the scoping. The shrine was instantly brought into view and he noticed arrangements being made for security but he was far away enough not to attract the attention of the police. That was the whole point of this sniper rifle to allow a hit from distance outside the ring of police that would surely be there to guard the two dignitaries. It took three bullets so the second shot could be done almost before the security services knew what had hit them. The shrine was nothing more than a little park which would be teeming with people come the 15th. He would have to get the faces right of the emperor and Prime Minister else the whole exercise would be wasted. He packed up the rifle and debated whether to leave it in the room thinking it very unlikely the police would do a search this distance from the shrine.

He decided to leave it in the room hidden under some boxes. He dusted himself down and exited the building in the opposite direction to the shrine. He would be back at 12 o clock on the fifteenth. He had three bullets but knew that two should do the job. His finger prints were not on any data base so he did not fear the rifle being discovered, although obviously anything could happen. He made his way back to the safe house and there were Sonny and Gustav eagerly awaiting news of things.

"I found an old high rise building a couple of blocks away from the shrine. It was ideal cover as the police would be unlikely to look there, The festival opens at two 0 clock which meant I should get there by 12 0 clock," said Ishai calmly. "Our plan is looking good. We get the hit done which will cause pandemonium, and lead to every security conscious person in the city on the look out. I should have plenty of time to get away. The only problem is do I leave the sniper rifle or risk taking it and getting rid of it. If it is found in the old building the security services will quickly see an Israeli connection which may lead to our detection. I know we have all got false papers and identities but there was nothing about Israel being involved and there maybe those back home wondering who this renegade is. Once back at the safe house we will have about two or three hours to get the helicopter and decimate the skyline. You get a good fast car Sonny to take us from the Meiji-jingu gardens.

"Yes," said Sonny breaking from his concentration. "We will then have to go into hiding until the time is right to do the Factory Whaling Ship. Whilst Japan is a well populated Island it will not be easy keeping out of the limelight once we do the hit and the skyline damage. We will have to move somewhere, maybe even leave the country but that will be nigh impossible due to blanket security checks."

"Maybe we could go to the north of the Island to the Whaling ports and hide up and prepare for the finale," said A Gustav full of

109

fire and concentration. "We could find a lot more to help our cause there."

"I wonder how Tanya is holding up," said a thoughtful Sonny. "We will need to keep in touch and she has been doing little except looking at your drawings of a Whaling Factory Ship. She is so enamoured to this project, said Sonny casually. "And I like the idea of hiding in the Whale ports. I will get on the computer right away to arrange a place there. I have friends around the globe who can arrange almost anything. If we hole up in a whaling port it puts us right in the place we need to be to find out information. Even though the pressure of hiding from our misdeeds will be considerable it can be done. At the moment Adolfo and his team are thinking the events before were the work of the 'World Caliphate' so for the time being we are relatively free to do as we please. Just when Adolfo will realise he has been set up is anybody's guess, but it gains us cover and time. He knows a green terrorist organisation has also claimed responsibility but as of yet knows little else about us. We are one step ahead of the world's security apparatus. The Day will soon come when the whale can calmly swim in the world's waters free of the harpoon in its back. I guess or wonder if our actions in Japan will be linked to the other events we carried out. Adolfo will probably guess that I am the man behind it all and then even think that it has something to do with whales. Adolfo always thought me something of a nutter but as I have argued earlier think we have a noble cause. I don't know if they have the death sentence in Japan but we will be on top of the Japanese people's hit list once we have carried out the acts in the next few days. I know that in Japan there are some good people who believe in preserving whaling stocks for whale watching but drastic action is needed to stop this barbaric and pointless culling of our time lords of the oceans. Whatever the outcome is for us we will be judged ultimately by the whales themselves as maybe they can cheer for us, as we save them. I don't think that there is much more we can do, as for sure we cannot do everything. Our actions will shake up the world's elite for a while and I am sure that many millions of people will be on our side. This is not a religious escapade. It is meant to stop the process of whaling by the world's governments and hopefully we can succeed. We will need to get our point across to the media after we have dealt a death blow to one of their factory ships, ships that spell death to so many whales in the name of scientific research. We are trying to bring about a new order to stop the genocide of planet earth."

"Whatever happens we three are with you all the way. Ishai has good reasons after his wife was blown up and me and Tanya love animals. I will go down in history for sure" said a Gustav full of delight. Tanya added, "We've done well so far not only to evade the security services but to stir up the world's populace with our daring deeds. I doubt if Adolfo thinks that we are in Japan waiting to strike the Prime Minister and the Emperor. Two days to go. You will need to rest tomorrow and be up early the fifteenth. While you three are away I can found out about the Whaling town of Shimonoseki in the north. Sonny has been very fortunate to date with contacts finding places to stay but soon we will virtually be back on our own. It will be hard finding a place to stay especially as there are four of us and there must be pictures of us in the papers soon after Adolfo rumbles the 'World Caliphate', and finally get his security apparatus working again after our hack. As we are not Japanese we will stick out like sore thumbs for a while, so maybe a better idea would be to leave Japan and come back in the Spring.

Sonny stood up and addressed the other three," Yes it will be very difficult for us as all foreigners will be seen as a threat after our assassination on the 15th. The question is where do we go when the skyline venture is completed and that will cause mayhem too. Everyone will be on the look out for us. We could split up and go our own ways for a while and meet up in the north whaling port in a few weeks separately. That would seem the most natural thing to do and then there would be all the paper work needed for your identities and money arrangements so that you can survive." Ishai said he had contacts a plenty who could provide cover for him, it was just keeping Adolfo off his tail that would prove exacting. Gustav then added, "Suppose one of us gets caught or all of us what do we do then as we would be in deep shit without finishing our mission and letting the world know through a statement our intentions which I am sure many millions will share a sympathy with." Sonny replied, look at it like this we've been successful so far. The world will look upon our adventure. It is for them to judge. We are clear of detection so far but the world does not know what we are fighting for as I was going to release a statement via satellite after we have taken the Whale Factory Ship out. Countries like Japan they place so much in their whaling ships. They like to lord it over the seas, to sort of assert themselves probably as a result of what happened at Hiroshima and Nagasaki. They have an inferiority complex to date. We are four humble people, who think it is time a permanent halt to whaling was achieved and which should be achievable by democratic processes. The fact that governments cannot bring about a cessation for ever in whaling to prevent extinctions allow a group like us to stand up and fight and be courageous. I have plenty of friends in high academic circles who can organise false identities and arrange payments. It is just the sheer scale of our actions which puts us right in the public eye. Maybe we could dress up as Japanese people after all the infamous James Bond played by Sean Connery turned into a Japanese character for a while to infiltrate a criminal network. In fact I think that that maybe the best way forward. I can contact my friends in America via my secure computer link up and get false identities in days. What do you think?"

Tanya said there would be language barriers to overcome.

"Yes, but if we went out alone we would not have much to say anyway," Sonny tried to reassure everybody. "At least we would not look foreign and attract attention. After the hit on the Emperor we cannot come back here. Local people will have seen us wander about even though we have been careful, but there will be a full scale witch hunt. I don't know if both the Emperor and the Prime Minister are popular but in any event it will not matter as the entire security apparatus will be looking for anyone and especially foreigners. And people talk and tell the police they have seen a group active in the wholesale district. It offers quite a problem for us. Ishai said that there were ways of covering the face up and that he would be wearing a mask for the helicopter ride on the city skyline, to stop himself being photographed from the many ways to do that. Gustav was clean shaven and wondered if his name had appeared under the Adolpho radar. He looked so different than when he had first met the others with his long beard and hair. He figured a mask too would be needed, just to stop the other helicopters that would certainly attempt to track them from taking pictures to feed back to the authorities. Ishai told him that he had a few. You simply pulled them over your face and there were eye holes to look through. Remember, they had info on us in that hotel in Kensington. I am glad that hack went well as their entire system was put in to a state of chaos. With pictures going missing and false information being placed in to security data bases.

"Well," said Sonny for sure Adolfo and his team will be up in arms when they hear of this hit in Tokyo and will probably then connect the events to me. Adolfo had a dossier on his time in the Colorado psychiatric institute and knew how dedicated I was to saving the whales. They are likely to put two and two together and figure that I was on a mission. But the mission will almost be completed. What I want is to be beamed onto the world's televisions after the Whaling Ship has been taken care of and explain my self and my views. But I have explained them to a hardened Israeli and he was won over so it is likely that the authorities will try to stymie that fearing that I could change the established order of the world. Whilst this talk had been taking place Tanya had been making a vegetarian dish of Mushroom Stroganoff. And said it was time to eat. They sat round the table in the centre of the room and awaited the treat. Their computer was switched on logged into a news channel and others to see the current situation. The reports of what they did before they reached Japan were still high on the news agenda but tailed down a lot. They ate and were happy.

"Here's to Leviathan," said Sonny.

"To leviathan", the other three raised their fists.

CHAPTER 17

The morning of the 15th came and they were all up early, listening to the news channels, the ones in English anyway. They mentioned that the Prime Minister and the Emperor would be visiting a shrine today along with some children to commemorate something connected to the Second World War. This was to be at Two o clock. Sonny told Tanya to look up in her computer later tonight to see where they were. As Tanya was not going to Tokyo she had to clear the place up and find somewhere else to stay. Adolfo, Gustav and Ishai loaded up the car, a modern looking Toyota bought and paid for, not hired. It was early 6 o clock in the morning and Ishai new from experience that it was going to be a very long day. Ishai told Gustav that he would have to pick up the helicopter after the hit from a disused airfield on the outskirts of Tokyo. Time would be tight. He would have to use the underground. Gustav would have to come along with him so he would need to meet after the hit. The Tokyo tower he suggested as a meeting place. They would then both ride the underground to the airfield and begin the carnage on the buildings of Tokyo. The micro-Uzis would be waiting for him in the helicopter. All Gustav would have to do when Ishai encircled the skyscrapers in the helicopter was hang out and fire the micro- Uzis into the vast glass window frames.

This would probably last about ten minutes during which carnage should have occurred to all the major buildings. But there was likely to be substantial security services activity due to the hit so we would have a small time line of landing the chopper in the park and for Sonny to drive us off. It is all about the element of surprise here and efficient machine gunning of the glass frontages of the skyscrapers. It would round off the day.

It was a quarter past six in the morning, and the car was almost packed. It would be a long drive from Kanazawa to Tokyo, taking four hours, but Ishai had left the sniper rifle in the disused building so he would not have to worry on that score. They set off for Tokyo at half past six in the morning wishing the best for Tanya who had her own laptop with secure access codes to tap into the others lap tops to keep in touch undisturbed from security apparatus. She said she would look into accommodation and other things in the northern whaling ports.

Ten thirty and the three eco- warriors were back in the wholesale district of Tokyo. A four hour drive. Ishai had a small holdall which he contained a mask for the helicopter ride. He reiterated the meeting place for Gustav at the Tokyo Tower, and told Sonny not to be late for meeting the landing of the helicopter in the gardens and set off to the disused building over looking the shrine. The shrine celebration was not until two o clock so he had plenty of time to get there via a circuitous route. He did not want to fall fowl of any police road block they might have. He found his sniper rifle as he had left it and assembled it. He looked through the dirty window and could see over the site of the shrine. He lowered the window and rested the barrel on the tripod frame and looked through the high powered scope. He brought into view some faces of people meandering by the shrine and was amazed at how large they looked. The scope had the added bonus of facial recognition, and this meant that if you lost sight of the target you could quickly regain contact. It was now One o clock with an hour until the hit. He decided to take out the Emperor first, quickly followed by the Prime Minister. He knew the security detail would try and protect the Prime Minister once the first hit had taken place. The Rifle took three bullets and he knew he would only need two shots, and then he would leave. He decided to take the rifle with him when he left and dump it in a bin some place.

13.50 p.m. and the dignitaries arrived making a fuss at the entrance to the shrine. There were a lot of people no doubt wanting to glimpse the Emperor. Ishai had by now pointed the barrel on a raised crate looking through the window down the street. It was quite a distance to the shrine, possibly half a mile, but it was the only place available for the hit. He looked down the scope which was programmed with the correct facial recognition data and picked out the head and face of the Emperor. Although he was surrounded by other functionaries it was a clear hit. The he scoped the prime minister not far away form the Emperor. He decided to get it over with a quickly as possible. He was on a mission like any other. Within a few months he would be finding out the secrets of the Japanese Whaling Factory Ships. He rescoped the head of the Emperor and when satisfied he could get a good shot fired. Continuing looking through the scope he found the head of the Prime Minister and fired bullet number two. Then he took time to scope the result. It looked like hell had broken out with security guards fighting to protect the leaders. Ishai, however had no time to lose and disassembled the sniper rifle, put it in its bag and then left the building as stealthily as possible. He closed the window and moved the crate away so as not to make it obvious someone had been there. He could hear police sirens but as of yet he was far enough away to make his escape. He would know later just what damage was done and whether he had been successful. He passed a restaurant which had huge bins by the side and casually threw the sniper rifle away. He walked on with his holdall bag over his shoulder and made for the nearest metro to meet Gustav at the Tokyo Tower.

Meanwhile back at the shrine the Emperor was dead with most of his face missing and the Prime Minister too. There were scenes of mayhem as the security services wondered what to do. Straight away they put up a cordon around the shrine and put a search into operation. It would not be long before the building that Ishai used would be found. The security services tried to hide the news of the deaths to stop panic, but inevitably in the age of mass mobile phones people were relaying their friends and the media about the murders. But by now Ishai was deep underground and well away from the scene. Someone may have seen him on his way but they would not be putting two and two together just yet. It was not long before he arrived at the Tokyo Tower tube and met Gustav. No one seemed to be aware of the enormity of what had just happened, so the packed area was nothing that Ishai nor Gustav had to worry about. Nobody was looking out for them. Still it would not be long before holy hell hit the Capital with every single police officer and security force scouring the streets of Tokyo. Ishai had done a clean hit with the minimum of fuss. The state of the art sniper rifle had done its job efficiently and lay at the bottom of a restaurant bin and with a bit of luck would not be discovered. All they had to do now was get a tube out to the old airfield to see the helicopter and they had plenty of time to do that as it was only 15.00 hours. They were not scheduled to strafe the skyscrapers until around 20.00 hours when it would be firmly dark and the challenge of piloting a helicopter over Tokyo gripped Ishai. Meanwhile Sonny was watching the news in the flat in the wholesale district and there was to be success. Both men died and the police had sealed off the shrine area and asked the public to report anything suspicious to their nearest police station.

CHAPTER 18

An emergency session of a security conference was taking place in London. Adolfo was there as were the others. Robert Crowe slammed his fiat down on the table and shouted,

"What the hell was going on with the world. We have the Christ the Redeemer statue blown up causing absolute mayhem amongst the catholic world. We have a freemason building blown up in Germany hitting the heart of how our society runs. We have a major racecourse violated in which many people were injured and then we have an Indian business Magnate killed. Something is going on which we are not picking up. We do not know for sure who we are up against. And now within the last couple of hours we have news that the Japanese Emperor and Prime Minister have been assassinated. Mary what have you to say on this 'World Caliphate'.

Mary Simmons momentarily flushed at the anger of Bob Crowe.

"Well we now think the whole World Caliphate thing is a cover. Our files were hacked for a while and things were haywire. We have re-established and reorganised our files and think it may be this Sonny guy after all. We finally got the pictures of them at that hotel in Kensington and there were four of them. We think one of them is called mad dog Gustav a animal liberationist fanatic. Then there was the girl whom Sonny met in Iceland. The fourth figure we do not know. We think they are on some ideological battle with the world over pollution and things like that thinking that the planet needs saving."

"So what are we doing about it?" shouted Crowe.

Adolfo intervened. "I've known this Sonny guy for a long time. He has obviously finally put some of his mad schemes to work. He was nuts on saving the whale. When he was in the psychiatric institute he would ramble on for days at a time about how man was bringing whales to their extinction. Personally, I think he has been planning this for a long time. He sees himself on a mission. Now he's gone a step too far with the assassinations. But it means he is in Japan which we would never have guessed. I have contacts there within the Japanese business community who ask me to be on the look out for such people who are religious in their cause about saving the whale. I regularly talk to the security advisor to Draxon Pharmaceuticals, a Suto Suzuki to keep him up to date. Maybe it would be good to contact him."

"We will need to contact governmental security agencies first and get some pictures out there so that they know what to look for," said Bob Crowe a little more calmly. "It amazes me how one man can put a spanner in the whole of our security system with the 'World Caliphate' attracting out attention for so long. Are we sure that these four in this pictures outside the hotel in Kensington are involved. He must have massive help from somewhere.

Adolfo butted in. "He knew most of the top academics in the cetacean field and with a bit of planning could easily get these people to pull strings and get access to top secret computers. He has successfully evaded out detection for over two months, but like all terrorists they leave mistakes and trails eventually."

Mary Simmons added that, "But what will they do next? Surely they cannot take on the entire governments of the world. No one is capable of that. More than likely they want to leave a message to the world to show that there are some green environmentalists who can carry out such draconian acts in pursuit of their goals. But why no statements or such. We've only heard from the this fake 'World Caliphate' and that now that has been discovered maybe we will get a statement from this Sonny. These pictures we have of them are not brilliant and Gustav used to have a beard with long hair. It may take a while to feedback. But we have some rather grainy pictures of Sonny and the girl from the International Whaling Conference. I will get them sent to the Japanese authorities right away. They say that they have found the place from where the hit was made and that it must have been quite a sniper rifle to go that distance. They have not retrieved the rifle yet and have no reports of people being seen near to this building. We must act fast because we do not know what they have got planned next. And we know their capability. We do not know if they will be coming back to Europe to continue their atrocities, but it will get very hard of them to travel once we ship all the relevant details over. As for this mysterious fourth character we have no idea. None. It could be anybody but we are raking through Sonny's known contacts over the past five years. We will have a permanent link with Japan from now on but this is likely to cause an outrage throughout Japan and the world. We cannot have the world's leaders being assassinated willy nilly. It is bad enough so far with what they have done. We seem to be well behind capturing these four terrorists because that is what they are. We have underestimated them. When we capture them we don't want the public thinking them as Whale martyrs or something like that."

"Right," said Bob Crowe," we will give all the details to the various governments. And it looks like we have won the battle of the hacking, but just in case get your experts to write new security software. We don't want all of this being hacked again."

Meanwhile Sonny was watching the news and although the operation was a total success it was nothing without any statements to release to the governments or the security services. It was his plan to release statements to the world's press when the final stage of his scheme to free the whale had gone off. This could even be on top of a Whaling Factory ship but he was by now totally committed. He would be seen as mad, he knew by the authorities yet for sure there would be s enormous public support. It would all come down to how well he worded his statements to the world. But it seems that from what he could gather their cover had been blown. On the news right in front of him on the English speaking channel it said that four people were wanted for questioning about the events in September and October and especially with the most recent assassinations. They were said to be animal liberationists fighting for the whale. Sonny now knew that he would have to disguise himself as a Japanese person. He would have to let Tanya know too because he did not want catching for at least another four months when the whaling season took off. He got out his lap top and e-mailed Tanya. Tanya answered that she too had been watching the news and would have to go into disguise. This she said was no problem. The problem would be keeping in touch and finding a place to hole up for the attack on the Whale Factory Ship. The whole world would be looking for them but they had friends Sonny said in the extensive Japanese environmental movement. They should be able to provide a sufficient hiding place. He would immediately alert and contact them. Ishai and Gustav were about three hours off the next phase of the plan and they would be wearing masks in the helicopter. Sonny released a statement saying the pigs that lead Japan had been assassinated for continuing whaling. Only when whaling was banned for good would their actions cease.

Sure enough Ishai was sat in the helicopter with Gustav at the disused airfield. It seems Ishai's contacts had been more than obliging as the helicopter they had was a very modern one and one which he had piloted before. All they had to do was wait until 20.00 hours and then take off for the skyline of Tokyo. Ishai also checked the micro- Uzis as this was the preferred method of causing mayhem to the glass frontages in the high rise buildings. Enough ammunition. They would be up there for about 8 minutes and then would have to land before the security services caught up with them. Ishai reminded Gustav that the Japanese were Nazis in world war to which Gustav said and now they were whaling Nazis. He said people need so much convincing of the wrong doing of their governments.

CHAPTER 19

Suto Suzuki was talking to Adolfo Heinlitz.

"What do you think we are paying you good money for Adolfo. You had this Sonny Preston on the radar at the Icelandic Whaling Conference but it seems you have totally lost the plot. Out company Draxon has a considerable financial outlay in facilitating whaling and the last thing we want is a bunch of latter day heroes ruining it all".

"I am sorry Suto, but it seems he is getting help from his friends high up in the academic world. It would have taken considerable brains to hack into out systems but that is what they did, and then they threw us all off track with this' World Caliphate' which has turned out to be a front for the group's activities. We are gradually getting to grips with things. Their pictures are now splashed all over the world. It won't be long before we apprehend them."

"That's good to hear but we have security teams ourselves and may have to get involved," said Suto into a nervous ear of Adolfo who did not want mercenaries fighting his battles.

"Let's not get carried away Suto. There's nothing here that I and my team cannot handle. We'll probably have them in days."

"You're saying not to get carried away, for Christ's sake they have just assassinated the Emperor and the Prime Minister of Japan, who was on our side when it came to scientific whaling. This group is on a mission and it seems clear that it is to stop whaling. They are fanatical in what they believe in and it is quite clear will stop at nothing to achieve their goals. I think I may alert some of my men to possibly hunt them down and kill them."

"These people need bringing to justice and our team can do that. I do not know if they have the death sentence in Japan but they are wanted elsewhere too. They have some explaining to do. I mean what else can they do now. We have them cornered in Japan. They will not be going far."

"With the liberal nature of many of the world's governments we cannot hope for a suitable punishment, that is why my own private security team will take them out at the first opportunity. We cannot have other groups of heroes taking up their cause. Your team have proven incompetent so far and I warned you of this Sonny Preston ages ago. He is very intelligent and won't be forgetting his incarceration in a psychiatric institute. It was research into dolphins which he did not agree with which got him interested in saving the cetacean world from what he saw as predatory man."

"Well, we would all like to know what really goes on inside those factory whaling ships, "said a curious Adolfo." It is no wonder groups get excited and cause outrages with all this secrecy."

"What is the position now Adolfo," said Suto.

"We have every available security force on top of this. Now that we have sorted the hack out we can begin to trace their movements but it is far from easy if they have false identities which they undoubtedly will have. We can only rely on the public for sightings of these four. In Japan they would be conspicuous and I am sure we will have their bases under observation before long."

"Well the business community will be going nuts over these assassinations as it will destabilise the country. A country needs its leaders. We have been through this whaling question many times and the conference voted for continued scientific research, so what have we done wrong. We cannot have eco terrorists ruling the day. Democracy is what we all believe in. Like I say our companies have considerable stakes in the pursuit of modest scientific whaling practices. We don't want these latter day eco warriors to win out. And for all that we know they might. The public is a gullible thing at times sympathising with this cause and that cause. My men will do a professional job and are entitled to do it legally as our company is under indirect attack from these thugs."

"You have that right to defend yourselves but don't take the law into your own hands. A proper trial can make these eco warriors seem ridiculous."

"It is not a question of taking the law into our own hands but of protecting our right to do business peace fully in a democratic nation. We've heard nothing from this group or had any statements issued so we don't know their further plans but it seems that they will stop at nothing to achieve their goals which we all know now is to stop whaling. To think that when this started with the Christ the Redeemer Statue, we had this Sonny Preston under the radar. He and his gang have got away with too much. And we know of his girlfriend that he met at the International Whaling Conference and we know of Gustav, someone who is prepared to die for his beliefs about the mistreatment of animals by man. The fourth character we know nothing about at all. But we could have, Adolfo, have nipped this in the bud if we had pulled Sonny in at the International Conference."

"Yes, it is all right saying that but what could we have held him on. We had no wind of what they had been planning and you cannot stop people travelling the world to watch whaling conferences. He's been planning this ever since he was released from the psychiatric institute. They will have a lot to answer for, as they said it was all right to release him."

"Well Adolfo I will have to go. Hopefully we will have this group under control before long whether it is to kill them or bring them to justice."

With that he rung off leaving Adolfo staring out of his office window. Adolfo knew little of Suto's activities but he had his own security force so he must be bigger than he feared. Then he got a beep from Suzie Adams, Sonny Preston 's plant in his organisation. She was a computer geek and had successfully delayed the sending of the pictures to key security agencies around the world. Whilst some pictures did get through they were grainy affairs shot by CCTV.

"Adolfo, We still have some computer glitches. The pictures that you requested be sent to Japan will have to be delayed for a while as the computer is again seeming to be hacked or breaking down."

"What. More trouble Miss Adams. I though you were a geek with computers."

"Yes, I did major in computer science, but it seems some sort of virus has infected all pictures taken around the Kensington Hotel."

"Well we know three of them, and it won't be long before the fourth member is known. We can run computers on their backgrounds and recent activities. Surely the computers were working for the Prix de L'arc de Triomphe. I mean so many computers and cctv must have been working on the day to have caught someone tinkering with explosives."

"We are examining the data now but as of yet they have not captured anything," said Suzie Adams nonchalantly. "We got the tip off from Kensington Hotel and they split up outside. They must have planned it all there and gone their separate ways. Then with help from people high up in the United States computer security industry covered their tracks. I am just sorry that we cannot give the Japanese perfect photos of the four of them. It is only 7 hours since the assassination and time is of the utmost. Is there anything else that I can do for you Adoflo?"

"You can try and track down this fourth character. Run him through facial recognition software. He must be known somewhere."

Although Suzie Adams knew Sonny Preston, even she did not know the rest of the gang and as for this fourth character, she would take her time. She was in charge of the computer section and security so she could interfere and slow down the operation at her will. She smiled at Sonny Preston's audacity so far in eluding all the security services of the world. Soon would be the revelation that we would know for sure what was going on in one of the Whaling Factory Ships. Something which intrigued her all the time. She would do her best to stall the search for them and at the same time put across a clean image of innocence. Adolfo the fool that he was suspected nothing.

CHAPTER 20

Ishai and Gustav were sat in the helicopter. It was time to go. They did not have long to be in the air but wanted to do as much damage as possible. He switched the machine on and when it had warmed up he took off and headed for the Tokyo Tower in the dark. Though with the neon lights of the skyscrapers and the Tokyo Tower it was a sight to behold. Ishai handled the helicopter with a dexterity that only members of the armed forces knew how.

"We will soon be at the tower. Do you see it over there in its orange glow. What you can do is strafe the restaurant towards the top and then we will go over some skyscrapers and strafe all the glass frontages. Just enjoy yourself Gustav. And sure enough they were upon the Tokyo Tower looking straight into the restaurant, when Gustav got out a micro- Uzi and began to fire at the windows. Some diners were wondering what was going on and began screaming when the glass shattered. Many ducked for cover in the vain hope of missing the bullets. The noise from the gun. The smashing of the glass it was ecstasy for Gustav.

"They won't be easting whale meat tonight Ishai," shouted Gustav as he rattled off the machine gun with its thousand rounds a minute. Then Isahi swung the helicopter away from the Tower as enough damage had been done there, and headed for some skyscrapers lit up by green neon lights.

"You may need to hang out the door to get a better aim Gustav," shouted Ishai.

"With these beautiful machine guns I cannot fail to hit the windows," and there was a sound of glass crashing all around them." The equation was simple a bit of broken glass for each drop of blood spilt by Leviathon, or so reasoned Gustav who was in his element. They strafed four skyscrapers and then Isahi said they would have to get out of there and meet Sonny. There was no body chasing them in the night sky, as it was too early for the authorities to fully understand what was happening. They were only up there for about ten minutes and Ishai was already hovering over Meiji Jingu gardens.

"Nice bit of work Gustav. That should stir things up. Forget about casualties as they could not be helped, but hopefully there would not be too many but we were at war thought Ishai. The helicopter was shut down and Gustav and Ishai climbed out and met Sonny with the car. They climbed in and sped off listening to wailing police sirens in the distance. They had made it. The security services were not quick enough to get a helicopter up in the air and could only watch from afar. By the time they found the helicopter in the gardens they would be long away.

"We've been pushing our luck so far on this mission. We are so close to finishing it. Now come the real problems. They have by now our pictures and our names. As you can see I am in the disguise of a native Japanese with dark skin and all. I suggest you two do the same. If we are to be successful in the rest of this mission we must be prepared to hide. I have friends and contacts in the Japanese Environmental movement. Not all Japanese believed in the philosophy of Scientific Whaling. So we could stay underground for quite a long time. In fact I am driving to a person known as Kuki now. She has a house prepared for us later in Shimonoseki, a whaling port where the Nishin Maru research ship is docked. Sonny now was in the hands of this Japanese environmentalist. But he had full confidence in her abilities to hide them until the spring. She knew what they were up to and supported their cause wholeheartedly.

On the drive there Sonny was telling Gustav to e-mail Tanya. But he was having no luck getting through. They were wondering if something had happened to her. And sure enough she had been picked up by the police. Although dressed as a Japanese woman, someone had grassed up the place where they had been staying in Kanazawa. Probably the group had seemed suspicious the more so since the Emperor and the Prime Minister were shot earlier that afternoon. Their pictures were displayed on all the television stations and someone local must have tipped off the police., though the pictures were rather grainy. She thought that she had got away all right after dressing up as a good looking Japanese woman which was not that hard to do. She knew that the other three would not be coming back to Kanazawa so with only her lap top which would be used to make contact with the other three, she left the house, after tidying up, for good at around mid afternoon hoping to find a place to stay in a whaling town in the north. She had stayed long enough to get the news on the hit by Ishai and was glad it had gone successfully.

She had scoured the net for places to stay but realised that Sonny had friends in the environmental underworld of Japan who could be called upon. She had no names as such and was searching in the dark. She would e-mail them later. She had plenty of money to get by and desperately needed a place to stay for the night. She found the town called Shimonoseki, a whaling town in the north, where some of the leading Factory ships were harboured on the internet. She figured on heading that way and finding a place to stay. It was while coming out of the house at Kanazawa at around 16.00 hours that she sensed something was wrong and as she headed down the street three detectives in the Japanese police force picked her up and said she was being arrested and was asked where were the other three members of the gang. She played all innocent saying she was a college student from America studying Japanese culture. But the detectives were having none of it. They said she was part of a foursome that had caused havoc in the world and had only earlier today been involved in the shooting of the Emperor and the Prime Minister of Japan. Tanya was no fool but realised they must have good intel on the gang and that all the hacking by Sonny and his friends had now terminated. Their pictures were being circulated and it was a foregone conclusion they would all be picked up before the grand finale of blowing up a

Factory Whaling Ship at sea. And discovering what was really going on.

She denied that she was called Tanya Brown saying her name was Caroline Cramer from Oregon and that she had been in at the time of the shootings of the Emperor and the Prime Minister. As for causing terror around the world she shook her head in disbelief. One of the detectives called for back up to search the house where she had been staying. By now Tanya felt crestfallen. To be captured when the finale was so near in the Spring. It was November now and the winter was going to be spent planning the finale of the whaling ship. She felt like she had let the side down and she had her lap top with her too. They could not get into the lap top without a pass word so she had some respite. But her dream of making a statement in the Spring time after blowing up a Factory whaling ship was now gone. She saw little way out of her present predicament. She had been caught but she knew a brilliant court case would ensure allowing her to express all her vented frustrations. That would be a bonus. The police said that they were taking her first to Kanazawa central police station for confirmation of identity and the later she would be transferred to Tokyo for a proper interrogation. She was wanted in other countries too, for the Christ the Redeemer and Prix de l'arc de Triomphe atrocities. She said that she did not know what they were talking about. Then one of the detectives mentioned a neighbour saying four people, foreigners,. were seen staying in this house.

We showed pictures of the four wanted people to this neighbour and he said they looked like the four in question. So please don't waste our time with all this student crap. She said she had been living alone but had had friends around. But she knew she was done. She could not hide the fact that she was Tanya Brown and that she had been seen with three people to make up the four. What she had to do was do the best she could. She could not get a message across to Sonny without the detectives knowing and she could not bluff her way around as she could not speak a word of Japanese. But for the time being she maintained her story that she was an American student. After all, they had no proof of her involvement with the deaths of the Emperor and the Prime Minister, as she was there in the house at the time of the event.

She had no idea on how Japanese justice operated but she knew she should ask for a lawyer, whereas the police wanted to know the whereabouts of the other three. She finally said that she was doing no more talking without the presence of a lawyer. One of the Japanese detectives lost his temper and said,

"Look, our emperor has been shot dead along with the prime minister and you talk of lawyers, you'll be facing the death penalty for this."

But she was saying nothing more and sat in the back of the Japanese police car. They drove off leaving a watch on the house in case the others returned but somehow they doubted it, thinking that they would know by now that Tanya was captured, no matter how secretly they dealt with the matter. What they did not know was that Sonny's friend Kuki had meant to get in touch with Tanya about Shimonoseki and hide all four of them until the heat died down. One of Kuki's friends had seen the police arrest Tanya and told Kuki the news.

"That's bad luck said Gustav to the other two. I guess we were lucky to get away before they pounced. The police will be mad as hell over these two shootings. What will we do now, Sonny?"

"Sonny's strained face said it all. I guess the cat is out of the bag. We must have faith in Kuki to conceal us. There will be a court case with her and she was always prepared for that in order to have her say. She will be in her element in court. I know that there is a death sentence in Japan, but it will be us three that the authorities really want. She does not know where we went after Tokyo so as long as we can hide we can still set up the finale and go out with a bang in the Spring or even earlier depending when the factory ship sets sail. As of yet they do not know what more carnage we intend but that will make it more of a challenge for them to find us. For the time being they were staying with one of kuki's friends in the student quarter of Tokyo, as all exits were blocked due to the two killings. But to hide for a few months would not be easy. They must stay in doors and not talk to anybody outside of Kuki's circle.

Meanwhile Adolfo had got the information that the girl had been arrested though there was no sign of the other three. He was a man in a good mood feeling it was only a matter of time before the whole gang was reprimanded. Then he could begin to relax a little and sleep better. But what of Suto Suzuki? Would he take the law into his own hands and sort things out that way. He would have to persuade Suto from doing this. He knew that the stakes were high with him being promised a large sum of money for capturing the gang. He would fly to Japan on the next flight and interview this Tanya Brown who was claiming she was an American student called Caroline Cramer from Oregon.

CHAPTER 21

Bob Crowe had received the news of the capture of Tanya Brown, although nothing was confirmed yet, with unease. On the one hand it was good that one of the gang had been captured but on the other three members were still at large and could cause mayhem. At the table with him was Mary Simmons. Adolfo Heinlitz had telephoned them to say that he was flying from Europe to Japan to talk personally with Tanya Brown. Bob Crowe moaned because he believed that they were part of a team and that as a team results would be better. He did not like this bravado of individuality thinking that he, Adolfo, could solve things all alone. Bob and Mary were at a police head quarters in Munich and things in Japan were moving very quickly. He knew that virtually everybody who was anybody in the police world would want to interview Tanya Brown. He asked Mary if she thought they had the actual suspect as she was claiming to be Caroline Cramer an. American student. What if they were wrong! They had been before. And they knew little about Tanya Brown except that she met Sonny Preston at the Iceland Whaling Conference. Would they get anything out of her, after all they did not know for sure that this gang had anything to do with these terrorist plots. She would not wave her right for a lawyer so if she says little we are back to square one.

Mary said that the chances were that it was Tanya Brown as she was seen with three other men the day before. Pity we could not raid the house then but I guess the public like to be sure of their facts. Mary said should we go too. To visit her. Trouble is although they have committed terrorist acts else where, it is the Japanese authorities that especially have major interest in these four. They get jurisdiction first. It was now 10 p.m. at night on the 15th November. It would probably be best if we let the Japanese process her first. She can always be brought back to Europe at a later date. But there was the Brazil affair too to be thought of. Maybe an international court could be set up to try her. But in the mean time the Japanese are going to be mad as hell about the loss of their Emperor and Prime Minister. What I will do is get Adolfo Heinlitz to keep in touch and to brief them on the case. But little did Bob or Mary know that Adolfo had his own agenda because he wanted to find a solution for Suto Suzuki of Draxon Pharmaceuticals. Adolfo would go out in retirement a very rich man if he brought this gang of terrorists to book for Suto. Bob and Mary knew nothing of Adolfo's acquaintance with Suto. If they did Adolfo would be struck off from practicing as a police chief.

So the pair of them reckoned that they would have to sit tight and be kept informed of developments. If the police could break Tanya they might get the address or whereabouts of the other three.

So Adolfo was on his way to Japan and meanwhile Tanya was in a cell at Tokyo's central police station. There was an air of excitement about the place with the police talking of nothing else. All resources were to be expended on finding the killers of the Emperor and Prime Minister. The police were aware that the gang had committed other atrocities in other parts of the world so that other police agencies would want to question her. The first thing the police chief of Tokyo police station did was let the various authorities know that they had first fling with this woman. All else would be put to the back burner as the killing of the Emperor was too serious too let things slip from under their fingers. The police officer interviewing her was called Motasuto Motomachi. He was the chief of the police station. It was after 11 p.m. now and news of the helicopter raid on Tokyo's nightline had trickled in. It seemed the 15th of November would be a day to remember.

"So Miss Brown. Miss Tanya Brown where are the other three members of your gang", asked the police chief.

Tanya all defiant retorted,

133

"I do not know what you are talking about. My name is Caroline Cramer and I am a student of Japanese Culture. I have had some friends staying with me, but if you think they had anything to do with the deaths of your precious Emperor and Prime Minister you must be joking."

The police chief stared at her for a few moments and then said we will need the names and addresses for these 'friends'. You see we think that yesterday they drove to Tokyo and killed the Emperor and Prime Minister. Why they would want to do that is a question that I need answering. I mean what is your group claiming to be standing for"

"Once again. I am a simple student who is innocent of all complicity. How could I have anything to do with this when I was in Kanazawa. Its miles away from Tokyo."

"Yes, a perfect place or base to operate from, well away from Tokyo, a good place to plan things. Who are these three men? What are their names? Where are they now?"

"I wish I could help you but I do not know what you are talking about."

"Oh come now Tanya we have you in custody why stick up for the other three. You will get the death sentence for this."

"Well that's the end of your questions my lawyer just walked in. I have rights you know."

The lawyer was a woman who walked in to the interview room and said all taking with her client was to stop. The Chief looked bad tempered because of this and said he would be hoping to press charges of some description later tomorrow morning. The lady solicitor called Yushi Homato said her client would like a meal and a good night's sleep. We can discuss the charges tomorrow when it comes. But in the meantime leave us alone. The Chief of Police reluctantly left the pair of them in the room.

Yushi asked her whether she was Tanya Brown saying that she had to be truthful with her.

Tanya thought long and hard before answering the question.

"Suppose I say yes to that question, what will it mean for me."

"Well, as of yet they have nothing to hold you on. You have done nothing wrong. You have every right to go about your business free of police interference. I understand that you have been claiming to be called Caroline Cramer."

"Yes, I enrolled on a Japanese culture course at the University of Kanazawa. It is taught in English so there is no problem with the language. I did not want the authorities to know about me as I understand they were seeking me in connection with terrorist incidents. I know nothing about these incidents and decided to come to Japan for a break from Canada. My parents are wealthy so they can afford the fees."

"Do your parents know you are in custody in Japan?" said Yushi.

"No I don't think so. I prefer if they did not know actually. If you say they have nothing to hold me on then am I free to go?"

"We will see in the morning what charges they press. But the whole country is looking for a scapegoat for the murders. The police will be under great pressure and will try and bend the rules. Get a good night's sleep if you can after a meal and we will meet again in the morning. Sorry to keep it short but we will need to see what they try and charge you with, and it seems to me that they cannot have much evidence that you have done anything."

CHAPTER 22

Sonny, Ishai and Gustav were holed up in a safe student house. At this stage the less people that knew of them the better. They were talking of Tanya's arrest and what it would mean for them. Although they could still go ahead with their plan to blow up a Whaling Factory ship it would not be the same without Tanya. And more importantly what did the police have on the three of them now. The whole country and the world would be after them, but the time was not right to face the world. The coup de grace would be the statement to the whole world when the Factory Ship was successfully decommissioned. All they could do now is lie low and wait until most of the heat was off. They had three or four months to see through and wondered if they would be found out. They were in a comfortable house in the Shinjuku district. They would not be venturing out at all and would need all the help that Kuki could bring. They would make use of the time to plan the final stage of their plan to save the whale. The Factory Whaling ship the Nishin Maru was one of the planned targets. It was a huge ship supposedly used for scientific purposes. Sonny was itching to see just what was going on, on one of these huge ships. His mind shuddered at the thought. The Nishin Maru was anchored at Shimonoseki in the north of the Island, and they would have to get there. Ishai said it would not be easy getting explosives or anything hi tech due to police surveillance. He also was wondering if the police knew anything of their final attack. Judging by the news on the television the world was taken aback by the brutality of the gang's murders and the attack on the Tokyo skyline at night was the final straw. Appeals went out to the public to report anything suspicious and not to approach the three remaining gang members if seen. Much too was said of the capture of Tanya though there was talk of the fact that there was little evidence of her involvement. Sonny knew that Adolfo would be wanting to interview Tanya as soon as possible. As long as she kept quiet about the planned attack on the Nishin Maru they could still go ahead with their plans.

Tanya was in Tokyo now at the grand central police station. She had had a reasonable night's sleep and had eaten well. First thing next morning she found herself talking to this man called Adolfo Heinlitz whom Sonny had mentioned earlier.

"Come now Tanya you cannot keep up this pretence that you are a student called Caroline Cramer. We've been watching out for you ever since you made friends with Sonny Preston at the Icelandic Whaling Conference. What are you four murderers up to? Has Sonny got some gigantic plan to save the whale because he was ranting on about that during his time at the Psychiatric Institute in Colorado.? Come clean now and it will go down well for you."

"I've been instructed to say nothing because you have nothing on me. I am over here as a student of culture and I use the name Caroline Cramer to stop people latching on to my rich parents."

"But your parents will know of this sooner or later, their precious daughter becoming an international terrorist."

Tanya was defiant. "I am guilty of nothing. You have nothing on me only the ramblings of an aged security official who has it in for all youngsters. What am I supposed to have done?"

"Well there is the Christ the Redeemer statue affair, the freemasons bombing in Germany and the Prix de L'arc de Triomphe. We know you hang around with mad dog Gustav and Sonny but the fourth character we know little about"

"I wish I could help you but I am a simple student learning the culture of Japan."

"You are in deep shit Tanya and could get the death penalty. Murdering the Emperor and the Prime Minister. What prompted you to do that? Sonny no doubt aspires to be the Whale's saviour but he is a deluded mad man who should never have been released. I have dealings with Satu Suzuki of the Draxon Pharmaceutical conglomerate. I have been told to do what ever is necessary to capture this gang and bring them to justice. Just ell me where the other three members can be found and it will look good on your sheet."

"You seem to be deaf Adolfo. I have done nothing wrong and I know of nobody called Sonny or mad dog Gustav. So I do not know what you are talking about. My solicitor will be here at any moment and I do not know how you got a look anyhow. Yes I agree the shooting of the Emperor and the Prime Minister are nasty things but they were nothing to do with me. Then there was a knock on the door and the solicitor arrived. Yushi Homato wasted no time in telling Adolfo that he had no right questioning her client. And she stated that the authorities had no evidence that Tanya was responsible for the deaths of the two Japanese leaders. Adolfo at first protested saying she was a highly dangerous terrorist and that as Chief of Security he had a right to question her especially if future lives were to be saved. He understood that she was arrested with her lap top but that no one could get the password to gain entry to the computer. Experts were trying their best at the present. Adolfo said it would only be a question of time before the password was obtained and then we could see just what was on her lap top.

Yushi added that they could not touch her lap top without any evidence to suggest that she was part of this terrorist gang that was plaguing the world.

Would he please leave the two of them alone now. This has been a traumatic arrest and Tanya had every right to question the circumstances of the arrest. Yushi said that they had 48 hours to hold her after that if they had no evidence to charge her she would be free to go.

Motasuto Motomachi said that they were confident they would get the evidence that they needed to convict her saying that Adolfo had pictures of her with the other three from London, as well as pictures of her with Sonny at Iceland. It was just a question of refining procedures to make charges of associating with terrorists.

Motasuto wanted to know what they hoped to achieve, and Adolfo told him that they were probably trying to save the whale. This would mean that they probably had more events tucked up their sleeves. He needed more intelligence, more information. It seemed impossible to him that the Emperor and the Prime Minister could be murdered in the name of the whale and that there was no trace of the perpetrators.

It was now midday the 17 th Of November and Sonny, Ishai and Gustav were awaiting news of Tanya. Kuki had contacts that said she was being held at the grand central police station. For Sonny is was a loss they could live with. After all three of them could sort out the Nishin Maru. He told Kuki that they must have plans of this Factory Whaling Ship Port so that they could plan their finale. She said that she had contacts in the area and that she would do all she could. Kuki was a strong follower of Save the Whale and she would do all that it took to safeguard these three. She knew of what exploits they had done and was amazed at their sincerity to the cause.

"Rumour has it that they conduct some horrific experiments inside these factory ships", said a tearful Kuki.

Meanwhile at the central police station Yushi told Motasuto that she expected to hear from him within the next 48 hours to see if Tanya could in fact be held and charged. Tanya was left alone in a cell and was thinking of the other three and how close they were to their finale. The truth would come out as to what was really going on inside these Factory Whaling ships. In some ways she would not mind going to court to say her part about whales if need be. She was not sure if that was what Sonny and company wanted but it would help the cause of the whale if there was a huge media trial. There was no way she could reach any of the other three. She was amazed at the coolness and skill of Ishai, thinking of him as he aimed his sniper rifle at the two Japanese leaders. And then strafing the Tokyo night line with all that glass crashing down onto the Tokyo streets. They had caused enough mayhem world wide to register their point but nobody in the world knew what it had all been done for. Sonny had instigated these plans all in the name of saving the whale so she knew that the final part of the plot had to succeed for it all to make sense. Surely after all of this whaling would cease and then whales could freely swim without fear of going extinct as had happened to some species. She would have to wait to see just what was in stall for her, and hoping that Sonny and the rest of the gang did not get caught. She knew that he had environmental connections that would help the three hide until the heat died down. The trouble with Japan is that it was not a very racially integrated country. Foreigners tended to stick out. She saw in her mind this great trial but whether it would upset the plans of Sonny she did not know. It was just bad luck her getting caught like she did probably due to foreigners sticking out like a sore thumb.

Bob Crowe who was head of the security council wanted to know what Adolfo had achieved by talking to Tanya so rang him on his special number. Adolfo picked up and said that she was claiming her innocence stating continually that she was a student who used a false name to stop herself self being associated with her parents. Adolfo felt that this was all about the whales and that it could be their plan to bring about a total cessation to whaling with all this terrorism. This could mean that they had more plots to unfold. And with Tanya not talking they had no idea where they were. But it could not be easy in Japan hiding three European terrorists. They had her lap top but was informed by her solicitor Yushi Homato that they could not do much unless they charged her. Apparently they were thinking of charging her with belonging to a terrorist gang.

Motasuto Motamachi was seen pacing the police station uttering expletives to himself.

"These bastards are going to get away with this. We can only charge her with belonging to a terror gang but we have no evidence, just a couple of pictures. Her lawyer was quick to point this out. And the pictures are a bit grainy too so it is hard to tell if they are who we think they are. We think that a mad dog Gustav is one of them but the fourth person we know absolutely nothing about." It seemed that this Sonny has been seriously underestimated, and that he is getting help from someone with serious expertise. The hit was from an old factory half a mile away from the shrine the Emperor and Prime

Minister were visiting. They had not found the rifle. His job was on the line if they did not get results but this Tanya or Caroline Cramer as she was claiming was not in Tokyo at the time and could be living on her own. Only a neighbour saw her with three men only the day before yesterday but we have no pictures to go by. What would they do next? They had the audacity to strafe the skyscrapers of the city the same day of the assassinations. What a cheek and what does this say to our security services? If Tanya Brown refuses to talk and we get no luck with her laptop we may come up short handed. Trouble is the world's security services have been lead to believe that the group 'World Caliphate' were behind these atrocities and that most of the computer software had been hacked up to that point. So there have been few real sightings of any of these four."

Yushi Homato said that she would have to be charged within the next 24 hours or let go. And there would be an uproar from the public if they let Tanya Brown off the hook. Meanwhile Tanya Brown was wishing she could have her laptop back. She had a special code for wiping it clean. All she had to do was get it for a couple of minutes and that could be done. She would have a word with Yushi to see if it was illegal to hold it when she had not been charged.

Sonny, Gustav and Ishai were safely holed up in a student house. There was no way they were going out into the street, with their pictures being circulated on the world's media, regardless of dressing up as Japanese men or not. Kuki saw to it that they ate and slept well, and Sonny said that the heat would be on for four weeks or more, but that they were in no hurry until early Spring time in order to execute the final stages of their plan. Ishai had a detailed plan of the inside of such a ship and had to finish his report for the Middle Eastern Press as promised to the captain of the Nishin Maru.

"You know, Sonny," he finally said, I have to slant this article in favour of scientific whaling so do not hold it against me. It would arouse suspicion if I did not."

"As long as it does not lead to an upsurge in Whaling. The last thing we need is middle eastern countries siding with the whaling nations," Sonny replied.

"Thing is I made a deal with the Captain to support the scientific case for whaling otherwise I would not have been allowed to look around the ship, which brings me onto the planned bomb attack in the Spring. How are we going to get on board unnoticed? Surely by now your Adolfo will know what your real aim is and have all whaling ports watched with a high degree of security!"

"We have four months to make it good. We stay hiding here for a minimum of 6 weeks and then make our way to Shimonoseki. Hopefully by then we will have formulated a plan of action. Maybe we can get aboard one of their fleet by posing as cleaners. I know they expect their ships to set sail in tip top condition. Or we manage to get on board as stowaways somehow. Maybe a bribe of someone close to their security could help us. We have the money to do this.

Gustav, up until now was strangely quiet. He finally said that we must not let our cover be blown. "I know our pictures have been released to the media of the world but their quality is suspect. You cannot really tell who is whom. It is you Sonny they have under their radar from the Icelandic Whaling Conference. They may have me put into the picture too but Ishai is still, I bet, beyond their scope.

CHAPTER 23

It was now approaching the end of November, and Motasuto Motamachi had decided to charge Tanya with being a member of a terrorist organisation. They had pictures but Yushi the solicitor said the evidence was flimsy, with the police not being able to prove anything connected to the assassination of the Emperor or the Prime Minister. It was the opinion of Yushi that Tanya would get off after a brief trial. The trial was fixed for the middle of December. She advised Tanya to drop the Caroline Cramer bit, and she would argue in court that she was in Japan to study Japanese culture. The police had come up with nothing as regards the three friends that were seen at Tanya's house by the neighbour and Tanya said that she did not know them very well or where they lived. But police enquiries had not discovered the three and hence Motasuto thought it indicative that it was the other three from the photos outside the hotel Kennington, in London. Yushi explained that although Tanya had a lot of explaining to do the evidence was not there and to convict evidence was needed. Motasuto had thought that if she got off from the trial of following her every movement to find the other three perpetrators. It was imperative that they found them to stop further atrocities and to be tried for the assassinations. He wondered where this Sonny character was and his two side kicks. They were probably still in Japan. Every police officer in the country was looking for them. The stakes were high. They had not recovered the weapon that inflicted the damage, but they found the warehouse where they believed it was carried out. If only the security services had extended their safety zone around the Emperor, but still they were not to know that they were going to be assassinated. It must have taken quite a weapon to carry the attack out. There were no usable finger prints at the scene either. The terrorists had simply vanished into thin air. The strafing of the skyscrapers on the same day was audacious. We were only a few seconds behind capturing them when they landed in that park. Again there are no finger prints on the helicopter but micro-Uzi machine guns were found in board, and these were Israeli. He wondered therefore if an Israeli was involved. He would contact the authorities in Israel and see what they could come up with. They clearly had some military expert involved.

So there was Sonny Preston, an animal liberationist called Gustav and Tanya that they believed to be part of the gang. The last remaining person was seen in the pictures taken outside the hotel Kensington, but the pictures had clearly been interfered with. They must have someone working for them inside the security apparatus to cover their tracks, by altering pictures and generally obliterating evidence.

The trial of Tanya could bring them out of the wood work. If only we knew the real message of these assassinations and what they hoped to achieve. Adolfo Heinlitz was putting forward the view that they were hell bent on saving the whale. As of yet no proper statement had been released to the public of Japan to explain the murders, and that was two weeks ago. Motasuto did not know whether to release the idea that it was all about saving whales.

But Motasuto's job was done for him as Sonny released a statement saying that the Emperor and the Prime minister were killed for allowing Japan to continue whaling. The atrocities in other parts of the world were to let the world's authorities know that whaling in any form, especially scientific would not be tolerated.

"Do you think it was wise releasing that statement, Sonny," said Ishai.

"I did it to usurp Adolfo from doing just that. It was only a question of time that Adolfo would release a similar statement. Besides the world's public needed an explanation, and I was hoping to get much support from the general public. Now the public know where we stand."

"What about our plans to infiltrate a Japanese Whaling Ship," said Gustav, "they will know our plans now."

"They would have been watching the whaling ports anyhow, so our task will be just as difficult," replied Sonny who was wondering what Tanya was doing.

Then Kuki arrived with some more food and said that Tanya was going to trial mid December, charged with belonging to a terrorist organisation. Kuki added that Yushi Homato her solicitor said that there was a strong chance she would get off as there was no evidence save a few murky photographs. If she gets off she will probably be followed, so how would you get in contact?

"Tanya is integral to the plot to find out what was really going on in a Japanese Whaling Ship, so she would probably, if she got off, make her way to the port of Shimonoseki and then meet up with us. The whole whaling ports are going top be crawling with police and their agents. It is going to be hard and tricky, but we must see it through. Any ideas, "asked Sonny to the other two.

"I like the idea of bribing some officials. Money always talks and we have plenty of money," said Ishai. "We need to be finding out about who is responsible for the administration of the whaling fleets."

"I agree", said Sonny, "Money can buy anything. I will make some enquiries. Someone must be responsible for hiring and firing the crews to these ships and that is the person we need to bribe."

Meanwhile the media had been whipped up to fever pitch about these assassinations. A statement was released saying that someone was helping with their enquiries, but the people of Japan had been outraged that two major public figures had been executed. They knew that someone called Tanya Brown was going on trial in mid December, and there was much excitement about that. They were outraged that people from abroad could enter their country and carry out such assassinations. The strafing of the Tokyo Tower was the final straw. Many people in public were questioning the ability of its nation's security services to protect them. The pressure on Motasuto was incredible and he had almost nothing to show from all his team's work.

CHAPTER 24

It was Monday December 14th and the trial of Tanya Brown was due to begin today. The television programmes were full of nothing else, as was the case with the press. They were asking questions as to who was this mysterious Tanya Brown, and what motivated her? Tanya was aware of the statement that Sonny had released about non toleration of whaling, and she planned to have her say on the issue in court. Ten a.m. and Tanya was driven to Tokyo's central court. She was in a blackened out van and the swell of people outside the court buildings posed problems for security. Many photographers were there hoping to get a glimpse of this Tanya. Tanya was dressed in blue jeans and red bandanna. She was going to get her say on the matter of whaling, but she was optimistic too of getting off. The Trial was fixed to begin at 10.30 a.m.

She was kept in a holding cell until called up to the court, but she did not have much time to wait. She was brought into court and stood in the dock while the Judge listened to the charge brought against her of belonging to a terrorist organisation.

"How do you plead Miss Brown?" asked the Judge, a certain Moti Maserati one of the leading judges in Japan.

"Innocent" Tanya defiantly addressed the court.

There was a public gallery crowded to get a look at this enigmatic Tanya.

"Then let us begin," said the Judge.

Sonny, Ishai and Gustav were glued to the television at the time waiting for information on their friend Tanya. Gustav said that he hoped she would hold up to the strain of it all. The court trial was to be televised as the public was so outraged at the murders of the Emperor and Prime Minister but Japan was a democratic country and a fair trail must ensue. There were crowds outside the court house carrying placards that were mostly pro whaling.

The prosecution started off.

"Now miss Brown or Tanya did you not tell lies when arrested saying you were Caroline Cramer a student of Japanese culture. You see the prosecution alleges that you are part of a four man terrorist cell, responsible not only for the assassinations of our Emperor and Prime Minister but for certain terror outrages in Europe and Brazil."

"I sometimes use the name Caroline Cramer as a cover. You see my parents are very rich and I like the anonymity."

"Come now. Weren't you lying to protect your real identity"

"I've told you the truth. I was lawfully going about my business when the police arrested me on the whims of a neighbour."

"But you were seen with three men the night before the murders in Kanazawa. Where are these three men now Miss Brown?"

"I don't know what you are talking about. I had some friends round from the University and was having a few drinks. Nothing dangerous in that."

"But we know you are a green campaigner, is that not correct?"

"Yes, I am on the fringes and sometimes go to demonstrations against whaling and logging.."

"You've been captured on camera talking to a certain Sonny Preston at the International Icelandic Whaling Conference back in the summer. And we believe that this Sonny Preston has an agenda for saving the whale and that he is the ring leader of your group."

"I know no Sonny Preston but I meet many people on my travels in the green movement."

"You were seen at his hotel in Reykjavik where we believe you both planned some of the operations."

"I've been told I am good looking and I am only flesh and blood. I did meet someone whilst in Iceland but he said his name was Tim Patten. We certainly did not plan any terrorist outrages from there."

"We have pictures of you leaving a hotel Kennington in London in August and we think you were there with Sonny Preston and someone called 'mad dog Gustav' from Germany. What do you have to say about that?"

Tanya knew from Sonny that these pictures were of a very poor quality, as he had a plant in Adolofo Heinlitz's security apparatus who could suppress information so she boldly stated that she had never been there in August confidant that they had little evidence.

The defence barrister came forward and said that these pictures could be of anybody they were so poor. Then he asked Tanya what she was doing in Japan.

"I was a student of Japanese culture but I wanted at the same time to see first hand how the Japanese viewed the saving of the whale." At this point Tanya decided to go into a rant about the beauty of what she regarded as the time lord.

"You Japanese people have an inferiority complex over the second world war which makes you want to assert yourselves by hunting endangered species of whales. Whales have been around for millions of years and make man look like a dot in evolution. One of your prime ministers said that the whale was a mere fish. But think about it, if you can. Some species can dive 500 metres and resurface without getting the bends. Other species migrate half way round the globe from Mexico to Alaska. What would the planet be like without any whales which was going to happen if nations like Japan did not stop whaling. Many of the world's leading nations have stopped whaling and have even introduced whale watching trips." The judge intervened and asked for a psychiatric evaluation.

A psychiatrist came forward to the dock to give evidence. His name was Franco Ono and he was a Consultant Psychiatrist at the main hospital in Tokyo.

"Tanya has classic paranoid schizophrenia. She thinks she can talk to whales."

Tanya shouted out to the court" How can it be madness wanting to save ancient creatures from distinction."

The Judge said that the various conferences had voted for scientific whaling which was sustainable."

Tanya was seething and shouted back, "Japan has bought various nations votes with economic assistance promised. It is hardly fair. Some stocks of humpback and blue whales were so low that they will never recover. I do not know who is carrying out these terrorist acts but I am glad someone is fighting for the whale. I am being victimised just because I have been known to campaign with the green movement.

It must be remembered that the court was in the Japanese language and that translators were used. Sonny and co. were watching from the secure hide away and admired the stance of Tanya. She was convincing as having nothing to do with any group of terrorists. The defence barrister said,

"So you were here only on a sort of fact finding mission and to study Japanese culture."

"Yes, I wanted to know what made the Japanese so inclined to whale. I may even write a book about it."

"Your Honour," said the defence barrister to the Judge, "I request that the charges be thrown out. It is clear that there is no real evidence that this woman has anything to do with the assassinations or indeed the other atrocities carried out."

The judge said that a statement had been issued by the group responsible that it was intent on saving the whale and it seems that Tanya is also intent on that but I agree the actual evidence is flimsy. The judge then asked the Consultant Psychiatrist if she posed a danger to which the response was

"She would be all right on the correct medication."

The Judge Moti Maserati addressed the jury. There is little evidence that this woman was part of any terrorist cell, and the prosecution's case is flimsy. She is an active member of the environmental movement but then so are thousands of others. She was in Kanazawa the day of the assassinations so I fail to see how she could have been involved, so it is up to you the jury to decide on whether she is part of this gang which is terrorising the world presently.

The jury left the court and Tanya was lead back down to the holding cell to await the verdict. Gustav admired her stance in the court and was hoping and praying for an innocent verdict to come back. This would mean that they would be able to team up in the future, although it was certain that she would be being watched by the police.

Tanya was sat on the concrete bench inset into the wall of the holding cell anxious about her verdict. She knew it would be bad news if it was a guilty one. Yushi was with her and was confidant she would be acquitted.

"Even Japanese Courts have to abide by the law."

Two hours later the jury had reached a verdict and Tanya was lead back up to court to await the result.

The Judge simply said,

"Gentlemen and women of the jury have you reached a verdict?"

The foreman stood up and said "We have your honour."

"And what is it?"

There was Tanya gripping the edges of the dock with her hands all tense and nervous.

"We find Tanya Brown not guilty of being part of a terrorist gang. However we do find her suffering from mental illness which needs treating."

The Judge Moti Maserati said that he was imposing a court order that she be treated for her schizophrenia. The country of Japan could not have her wandering around calling the natives 'slant eyed.' Tanya thanked the court and the Judge and hugged Yushi. The media was in a frenzy that this woman had got off. Yushi said that the court order meant that she would have to report to a psychiatrist. As long as she did that she was free to do as she pleased. They would have to leave via a side door as the front of the court building was surrounded by cameramen and reporters all eager for a few words with this Tanya Brown. Also her parents now knew of her ordeal as it was relayed world wide and news outlets were eager for interviews. Headlines like "Legalised Assassinations" and "Schizophrenics can be dangerous" were rolling off the press. Sonny, Ishai and Gustav were thrilled to bits that she had got off. But how were they going to arrange a meeting. They did not know whether her lap top had been compromised or not but that would be the starting point.

Gustav was annoyed that someone wanting to stop whaling should be depicted as schizophrenic, as indeed he had been in Germany. It was a terrible label to have around one's neck.

CHAPTER 25

Tanya was booked into a hotel in Tokyo, hotel Okinawa. She had plenty of money so she used money in her real name from her parents funds. She was onto the them by phone from the hotel. Tanya's mother Irene was concerned for her daughter's welfare,

"Why did you not tell us you were going to Japan. We've been worried sick with that trial hanging over you. We are so relieved that you were found innocent else you could be doing life. Don't you think of your parents at all nowadays."

"Of course I do. I was just about to tell you both that I was in Japan when I was arrested. It seems that being green can attract the attention of the authorities."

Irene then said, "I do wish you would find a man and settle down to a normal life. All this wandering around the planet trying to be all things green was no good no matter how noble. Are you all right for money, because we can wire some over?"

"I'm doing adequately with your allowance that you both set up."

"So what are you going to do now? Surely you cannot stay in Japan."

"I have to stay a while longer as I am researching a book on attitudes to whaling. You know how much I am against whaling. Someone has to stick up for the rights of these creatures to swim freely in the earth's seas."

"But you have almost been found guilty in a court. Who are you hanging around with? Tell me you are not part of a gang besotted with saving the whale"

"No, nothing like that mum," Tanya assured her mother.

"Your father says if you keep getting into trouble with the authorities your allowance will be stopped, so you have been warned," said Irene emphatically.

"No, I promise I will be a good girl she said all innocently."

"OK we will leave you to your ways but please try and stay out of trouble. We have our good names to think of in the business world."

"Right-t-oh Mother, I'll keep in touch." And Tanya rang off.

Her room was a spacious modern affair with flat screen telly which she switched on. There was a discussion programme on the assassinations and some Japanese member of the audience was calling on the death penalty for the culprits. This reminded her that she would have to get in touch with Sonny to see how things were and for the latter stages of the plan with the whaling ship. The authorities had given back her lap top and she was pretty sure it had not been compromised but they could have put some kind of a bug in it. She knew she would be being watched day and night to see what she got up to. She only knew that Sonny and the other two were holed up with some friends in the environmental movement. Maybe they could reach her.

What was she to do now? She had to get in touch with the other three and prepare for the spring attack on the whaling ship. Gustav and co were thinking the same thing of how were they going to get in touch with Tanya not only to congratulate her on her court victory but to plan the next stage of the operation. Of course they could do it alone without her help which could be wise as she would be watched by the police and Adolfo Heinlitz.

Tanya decided to order some food and drink from reception, and waited half an hour before they arrived by trolley with a waitress. The meal was a vegetarian curry and as she placed the food from the hot plates to a serving plate she saw a piece of paper with some writing on it. It said quite simply Sonny Gustav and Ishai were safe and that she would be contacted again within a few days. She quickly destroyed the piece of paper and set about her meal of vegetarian curry and rice thinking of just how she was going to get in touch with Sonny and his two helpers.

Although she was free she felt like a prisoner as she was sure that her every movement would be being traced. She dare not try her lap top but she could buy another one as she had plenty of money.

Meanwhile there was a security conference with Bob Crowe, Mary Simmons and Adolfo Heinlitz.

Bob Crowe addressed the meeting and asked Mary what she thought of this Tanya, whether she was guilty of not.

"I would find it hard if she was innocent but to convict you need evidence and we have very little. Those pictures have clearly been interfered with. We have her under 24 hour watch and any contact she makes will be noted. So far she has just rang her parents and is staying in a hotel Okinawa. She seems to have plenty of money and as for the other three members, which we think there are, we have heard nothing or had no reports. They have vanished into thin air. How this could be after such atrocities is hard to believe. The public and the police must have seen something. And what have they go left up their sleeves. They must have something else planned. Adolfo says that Sonny when he was in the psychiatric unit, was obsessed with saving the whale so maybe they are doing something with one of those giant factory whaling ships. It would seem logical and we must therefore put out forces on guard in the whaling ports. We need a list of the whaling ports and of the factory ships that go on hunts. There cannot be more than ten such ships."

"We have the resources," said Adolfo, "to keep an eye on the ports. It seems entirely logical that they would aim for such ships but what they have got planned is anybody's guess. It seems incredible that they could murder the Japanese Emperor and Prime Minister amongst other things without detection, but then this Sonny has good contacts high up in Academia where all the best brains are. Many people don't agree with whaling so he must have huge support and he has spent three years planning this. Our best bet for the time being is for Tanya to make a mistake and get in touch with Sonny. I think it quite clear that she is part of this gang. It is just proving it.

We have a bug in her lap top which will tell us of any time she logs in but she has not used it yet. No fool is this Tanya she probably suspects that there is a bug in it. So all we can do is appeal to the public and keep an eye on Tanya until she makes contact.

"Yes," said a cautious Bob Crowe "But we cannot watch her all the time or control her actions. She will be onto the courts for harassment, after all she has been found innocent. I wonder if there is anything else we can do save wait for developments. For certain Sonny and his two helpers, one of which we believe to be 'mad dog Gustav', are not going to come out of hiding wherever they are and let us not forget they may not even be in Japan"

Mary Simmons asked when did the whaling ships go whaling.

"April for 6 months, said Adolfo "but they could attack some of the whaling ships in dock or at sea assuming they could get aboard."

"So we have got about four months to wait until the Factory Whaling Ships set sea," said a resigned Bob Crowe. "I find it hard that they can remain under cover till then. We have just got to hope that a member of the public comes across them like they did with Tanya. She was seen with three people the night before the murders but the trial did not actively put much stress on that event. Seemingly believing that she was a student in Japanese culture. But this has been going on since the Icelandic Whaling Conference in June and we may have our ideas on who is behind these atrocities but we cannot be sure. But the fact that Tanya a girl seen with Sonny Preston in June turns up in Japan at the time of the murders does, at least in my mind, imply these two are at work. As for 'mad dog Gustav' it sounds like something he would get up to with the added attraction of saving the whale from whaling. The fourth member we know little about but if he has had military training it will make the job doubly difficult. I mean it must have taken a military trained person to do the hits on the Emperor and the Prime Minister. And as for the strafing of the night sky line again someone had to fly the helicopter. But it appears they wore masks but micro –Uzi machine guns were used. We believe an Israeli could be involved and we have asked our security services to contact the state of Israel for assistance. So far they have not got back to us. They are checking their Data Bases to see if there is any renegade soldiers likely to latch on to the' save the whale 'cause. It is amazing that no finger prints were left o the helicopter but I guess they both wore gloves. Our own forces could not quite catch up with them as they sped away in a car, before we arrived at the gardens."

"What about Green groups in Japan? Have they been checked out?" added Mary Simmons.

Adolfo said, "That well known figures in the Japanese Environmental movement were being watched but that there were quite a few and nothing had turned up. It made some kind of sense for the Japanese Green movement to be involved. I'll cross check to see if any Japanese were spotted at the Icelandic Whaling Conference. But with such an extensive movement they could be kept hidden for ages. And then security services in Germany and Brazil want to be kept appraised. I just hope that have got nothing further planned around the world. The chances are that Sonny will go out with a bang in one of these Japanese Whaling ports to ram his message home."

Meanwhile Tanya went for a walk out of the hotel and straight away noticed some under cover police officers following her. She thought of contacting Yushi to see if she could get a court order against these. After all she had to report to a psychiatrist, so she had not got off scot free. No doubt her psychiatrist would recommend mind numbing medication. But she had no regrets of having called the Japanese people slant eyed. The Japanese public were just as involved with whaling as the ship's crews, as they ate whale meat as some kind of delicacy. As for the message in the hotel she would have to wait for further advice and it may transpire that she would have to lose the detectives that were following her. This would not be easy as the detectives had everything to lose and the pressure was on the police to get results.

Motasuto Motamachi was infuriated that Tanya Brown had been declared innocent. He was now in fear of losing his job because after 5 weeks they were no nearer to finding the killers. He felt for sure that Tanya would be found guilty. But for now it would mean watching her 24 hours a day, on the assumption that she would contact the other three. He noted that her lap top had not been used yet, and hoped that the bug they had planted within it had not been compromised. His detectives reported the fact that she had gone shopping from her hotel and had made no phone calls from outside, with one call from her parents from inside the hotel. They noted that Xmas would be upon them soon and that would be a terrible time for more terrorism. Tanya thought too of Xmas and of her dogs in Canada. She would have to ring the caravan site and make sure the dogs went into kennels, which is the next thing she did. She hoped that the sadistic dog killers had been found but they were still at large. It was Mike the security guard that said he would look after the dogs, saying that he would be happy to oblige. He also, as by now he knew that Tanya had been in court in Japan asked her how she was holding up. She simply said that she had been found innocent in a court of law and that in many ways it was simply not safe to travel nowadays. Mike was glad she was found innocent not wanting to believe that Tanya was a big time terrorist. Mike said that the world was a crazy place with the attack on Christ the Redeemer a profound attack on religious people. But he was no friend of the whalers as well which put him in a tricky place, as he could well understand the anti-whalers fight.

It was now December the 20th and Yushi Homato her solicitor rang to see how she was doing.

"Well I am being watched all the time and I think that there is a bug in the lap top. What do you think I can do?" said Tanya somewhat resignedly.

Yushi replied,

"I think I can get an injunction against the police for harassment but it will take time to obtain especially as it is nearly Xmas and the new year. The Japanese do not celebrate Xmas like the rest of Christians in the west, as the main religion was that of Shinto. But there were many who observed it. If Tanya could hang on until after the new year then Yushi was confidant that she could pull the detectives that watched her hotel day and night off her case.

Sure enough Xmas went a long with new year and the authorities were nowhere in sight of catching the terrorists that had carried out the atrocities around the globe. Sonny, Ishai and Gustav were still underground being cared for by Kuki and her environmental friends, but the heat had substantially died down, and it was now January. Sonny had located an administrators name that dealt with the Whaling ships and made steps to offer bribes of over a million dollars. He felt sure that that would do the trick when it came to smuggling the four of them aboard a moored Whaling Ship. Sonny refused to believe that someone would not betray their comrades for a million dollars, but either way he would have to be careful making sure the payment was not put into operation until they were safely aboard. Otherwise they would have to think of something else and there would no doubt be high visibility security, as by now the authorities felt they knew what he was finally up to. But Sonny was determined to let the world know just what the Japanese were getting up to on these giant factory ships. Soon they would have to make a move to Shimonoseki to take up a secure base for a while. But they did not know if it was feasible to move or not from their present surroundings. They had been looked after well and Kuki's friends were a disciplined lot. Sonny guessed that they would have to move out at night time for the safest bet of not being discovered. It would be soon but still they had not made contact with Tanya whom they now knew had taken an injunction out against the police for harassment. It was due to be announced on state news on the 5th of January.

Meanwhile Tanya had discovered the bug inside the lap top and removed it by throwing it down the toilet. She felt sure she could now converse with Sony via her lap top. She would communicate first by code with a simple run of numbers so that Sonny knew she was trying to contact. Then Sonny could get his friends in the states to intercept anyone hacking in to their networks.

It was Sonny that noticed his lap top bleeping and saw the code number for Tanya. He immediately instigated procedures to protect the privacy of the contact, and then in a few minutes they would be in touch.

And then there was a beaming Tanya looking through the screen on Sonny's knees.

"How are you all?" she said happily.

"We are doing well and intend on moving out to the whaling port soon. Plan is to bribe some official into smuggling us aboard a ship. Will cost over a million dollars but well worth the spend. How we going to meet up?" said an inquisitive Sonny. "Bye the way, you were great in court, and it was a relief to find you were found innocent."

Tanya replied that the injunction was due to be put on the police today, but although she would not be followed legally she was in no doubt that she would still be followed even if it was by Adolfo's security team itself. So she guessed that the best bet would be to meet up in the whaling port and await the whaling season. She could join them there and then plan the actions aboard the ship." Has Ishai done his piece on the whaling ship for the Middle Eastern press," she asked matter of factly.

"Yes he has, and has really crawled to the Japanese over their love of all things scientific, suggesting that scientific whaling has all the answers to man's ills."

"You think he will get recognised if we are seen in the locality of the same Whaling Ship where he did his research."

"He thinks not as he was well disguised last time wearing glasses and with a beard."

"So what's the plan once we are aboard the ship? We could be there for a few weeks and will need food."

"I was hoping the administrator we compromised may be able to help us there, after all he knows who he can manipulate on board rather than we do."

Finally Tanya asked" Were they really going to blow the ship up or just expose what was going on?"

Sonny took a little time answering then said,

"It depends on what we find. If we find mad experiments then we will have to relay the details to the free world. There is a problem that if we blow up the Factory Ship how will we get off? But that would make an extra impact towards our goals of liberating the whale from extinction. We could e-mail the Rainbow Warrior to see if they could meet up with us. They could rescue us but it would be tricky getting off the ship."

"Well, you think hard the next couple of weeks. I will contact you again when in Shimonoseki. I will have to go now as the longer we transmit the more likely a hack. Give my love to Ishai and Gustav."

"Sure will," said Sonny and contact was disconnected.

It was then that Tanya had learned that her attempt at injunction against the police had been successful. For the first time in weeks she smiled.

PART THREE

CHAPTER 26

The weeks went by and Sonny, Ishai and Gustav began to relax more. It was now late February and they would need to make a move to Shimonoseki. They had heard nothing from Tanya since the last contact early January. They assumed that Tanya would make contact when in Shimonoseki. It was going to take all of their cunning and guile to avoid the authorities and get aboard a whaling ship, probably the Nishin Maru. They were moved one night the 25th February, by car and as it was over two months since the murders of the Emperor and the Prime Minister of Japan, road blocks no longer applied. So it was a straight forward drive up to Shimonoseki, where Kuki had more friends in the environmental movement to hide the three whale freedom fighters.

They were located not far from the docks of the ships but as it was dark nothing could be seen. Sonny noted that they must get in contact with Tanya which he could do in safety due to their superior encryption codes. As soon as they were inside the new safe house Sonny got out his lap top and e-mailed Tanya who replied immediately saying that she was in Shimonoseki and looking forward to meeting them again. She said she had been darting around Japan trying to throw off any watching security staff and was confident she had done. Obviously the whaling ports would be being watched and it was important that they did not get discovered so near to their finale. Tanya asked about the bribing of the administrator, and Sonny said it was going to happen within a few days. Hopefully they would be smuggled aboard the ship with a few helpers in the process and they could then take pictures of what was really going on in these vast ships. It may be that it was impossible to blow the ship up. They would have to wait and see. But that would be the best way to get home the anti- whaling message, he felt. But Tanya wanted to know how were they going to meet up with so much security, which would be on the look out not only for her but for the other three. She had paid up front for a flat in the centre of the city so no one got to look at her. She had plenty of money to do what was needed to survive. But she radically changed her appearance with glasses and a long brown wig. How she would get on to the ship as a woman would be tricky and highly suspicious no matter what was said to the administrator. No doubt they would be smuggled aboard in the early hours of the morning by 'friends.'

Sonny and company made their new place of hiding a sort of home sweet home realising that they would only have four weeks to go before boarding the ship. They would have to get Tanya to join them without being discovered. He would arrange for the payment of one million dollars to the administrator within the next fee days and had his email address. They thought it best if they tried to look Japanese so they could mix in better. Ishai had to locate explosives to blow up the ship or at least take some on board on the assumption that they would wire up the ship to be exploded. It would take quite a lot of explosives but there were some very high powered explosives on the market. He realised that the administrator would want guarantees that no harm would come of the ship's crew or the ship. Sonny had little choice but to lie. He assumed that there were life boats on the ship for eventualities. Maybe they should take over the Captain's cabin after a few days at sea and control the ship that way, by threatening the captain's immediate crew that piloted the ship. Sonny remained convinced that it was not rocket science taking over the ship as long as they all had weapons. But it was especially important that they found out what was going on in side the bowels of the ship with these deep sea monsters. Micro- Uzis again were the best preferred guns as they delivered thousands of rounds in a minute, and were relatively compact and light. Ishai would have to use all of his expertise to get the explosives and guns meaning he may have to make a trip back into Tokyo but they had plenty of time. Also Ishai realised that the police would be watching and asking all the known weapons dealers for information but money could buy almost anything. And especially silence.

It was now the end of February, and Ishai had been to Tokyo, driven by a friend of Kuki's. And Ishai was amazed at times of how nobody had betrayed them to the police or security services. Good to see that the environmental movement showed that their belief in all things whale paid dividends. Next on the agenda was Tanya meeting up with her comrades. Sonny obtained security clearance from his computer and told Tanya that a car would pick her up outside the town hall. He gave the colour and type of car over the computer and mentioned a password she could use when the car approached her. This car would bring her to where Sonny and the other two were staying. It would be great to see each other again. It was 12 o clock midday and the car approached the town hall where Tanya was waiting. She recognised the make and colour and when it stopped she leant towards the driver and said the pass word of Shalom. That was the all clear and Tanya got in to the car ready to rendezvous with the others. After a short drive past the docks and the moored Whaling Ships they arrived at the safe house. Sonny was extremely pleased to see her as were Ishai and Gustav.

"We are four once more," said a jubilant Gustav, who continued, "Say you look different."

Tanya replied, that the whole of Japan knew what she looked like so it was essential she changed her image. Sonny added that all of us must change to appear more Japanese. We have make up artists who can work wonders. When you go on ship chances are few questions will be asked. I am sure you can make yourself look masculine with the right clothes. Which lead Tanya to the most important question of them all,

"When do we board the ship and have you decided upon which ship."

"The Nishin Maru is the centre piece of the fleet and I guess all the security services, if they are watching will keep an eye on that. We could go for a lesser known ship. I think six Whaling Ships are taking to the seas. We have to rely much on the administrator's ability to put the security services off track. There must be times when these people check the ships and other times when there is the all clear. I will be e-mailing the administrator tomorrow with the money and cementing plans. We have les than a month to outwit the authorities, and beam to the world just what is going on inside of these giant whaling ships. And we will need to know the itinerary of each ship which I am sure the administrator will know. He will probably ask for more money but we have plenty. I know it is a bit flimsy relying on one man for our ability to embark on a ship but there is little we can do it seems. I see no other obvious way on to the ships without being detected. Ishai made a successful trip to Tokyo a few days ago to get the weapons and all we can do now is wait and see what the administrator comes up with. He will probably give us all false identities but even though we pay him well he will need to compromise other people aboard the ship. I gather these fishermen, as they like to be known are quite a proud lot so it won't be easy."

"The main thing," interrupted Gustav is to get pictures out to the world of what they are doing to these poor whales inside the ships. So we will have to hide away for long enough for the ship to make a catch of whales. Chances are the Japanese fleet are exceeding their quotas and catching whales they are not permitted to. We will have to document it all."

"And" added Sonny we have not heard of anything from Adolfo and company about us. I did get a report from a contact that there have been several important high security meetings but basically they are back at square one. They don't know for sure that we will board a whaling ship. They probably think that we will carry out more atrocities. So I intend releasing a statement to divert attention away from the whaling ports to give an inkling of where we are going to strike next. I think I will mention Norway as they still whale too and are as bad as the Japanese.

"Adolfo must be going spare about us especially you Sonny," said Tanya with a subtle hint of amusement.

"Me and Adolfo go way back. I wonder just what is going through his mind.

Adolfo was on the phone to Suto Suzuki of Draco Pharmaceuticals.

"You bumbling fool," berated Suto, "You've let the woman Tanya slip beneath the radar. We have no idea where they are. They might not even be in Japan. We have big stakes to play here Adolfo. You won't be getting your pension if you do not carry out your function and find these four."

"It was bad luck the Court acquitting Tanya of membership of a terrorist organisation but the quality of the pictures on offer left a lot to the imagination. They must be getting substantial help from top computer engineers and programmers in the States. We should not have lost her after she stayed in that hotel Okinawa. She discovered the bug in the lap top which we never could control or break into. But there has been a total watch at all the airports and sea ports with nothing turning up. I have a feeling that they are still here in Japan and that they intend one more atrocity."

"Well, if you want your retirement bonus of a pension you had better find out before it is too late. We in the pharmaceutical industry do not want a scandal. We support scientific whaling as we believe that it is necessary to do research into new types of drugs. But I myself have little idea of what is going on, on one of these ships, which the environmental movement would like to know. They call for more transparency."

"We are watching the Whaling ports but so far nothing has turned up. They must be getting substantial help for them to go undetected for so long. Four foreigners would stand out a mile in Japan especially with their details released to the public. All I can do is get all my agents to keep vigilance and hope a member of the public recognises them. Like they did with Tanya.

"I've got an eerie feeling over this like things are out of my control. I do not like things out of my control and nor does my corporation" said Suto guardedly.

"International protocol has to be followed. You cannot take justice in to your own hands."

"It is not a question of taking justice into our own hands but of safeguarding our industry. We had Tanya in our sights and we have let her go. We have no idea where she is but we are certain she is part of the gang, regardless of what the courts say."

"We do not have any real idea where they will strike next other than a feeling for the whaling ports. Sonny Preston was obsessed with saving the whale when he was in the psychiatric institute and it looks like he has gone much further with his dream of stopping whaling. What audacity to take out the Emperor of Japan along with the prime minister."

"We've got to stop them. The interests of the pharmaceutical industry are at stake as well as Japanese pride."

"We do not know if they are in the country. It is so long since we heard anything. They could be striking at any of the many whaling ports around the globe."

"They must be getting substantial help from somewhere. Have you not checked upon the many environmental groups in Japan who may be harbouring him," said Suto with a touch or sarcasm.

"There are so many environmental groups that it has proven almost an impossibility to watch them all. We have raided certain houses but to no avail. They are certainly well hidden. It is so frustrating especially when we had one of them within our grasp. We should have done better at watching Tanya when the court released her, but she got an injunction and found the bug in the lap top. We've had no success in intercepting any e-mails from her lap top. They must have some of the best brains in the world working for them."

"I am sure that the personnel of our pharmaceutical company are a match for these terrorists and their backers. We've got billions of yen behind us. But it seems our computer security men have been hindered all along. And yet Japan is a major player in the computer world. Supposing they get to a whaling port what is the worst scenario?"

"Well, we know they want to find out exactly what is going on with this scientific whaling aboard these ships, but they would have to get on board first. And they are well guarded. Or it maybe that their targets are completely different but what a cheek they displayed by strafing the high rise buildings in Tokyo after the assassinations. That took some nerve and they got away with it. All the glass is missing from the Tokyo tower and there were casualties too. It seems that this Sonny Preston is surpassing anything connected to the world of terror. He is mad of course which is why he was seeing a psychiatrist for so long."

"I told you when we saw him at the Icelandic whaling conference that something was up. But all we have got so far is a few grainy photographs of them coming out of a hotel in London. There is mad dog Gustav, someone who will die for his animal rights beliefs. But the fourth character is completely unknown. Just how they have managed to slip beneath the radar for so long is really quite something. Have you had any luck with identifying this fourth character," enquired Suto who seemed desperate.

"I am just about to get onto Bob Crowe. We think that there maybe an Israeli angle," Adolfo tried to assure Suto.

"These Israelis are experts in warfare."

"Well, I will leave you there Suto, but you can be sure that we are doing everything possible to capture these terrorists," said Adolfo attempting to reassure Suto.

"I hope so for your sake. Remember your pension is at stake if you do not stop Sonny and his gang meddling with the Japanese whaling fleet, if that is the intended target."

It was at that point that news came in of a statement released saying that Norway would be the next target. The statement did not mention any names or the recent trial of Tanya.

Adolfo let Suto know of this new development but Suto was sceptical as he thought it may be a diversion. "Well I will leave things with you Adolfo, but remember failure will come at a high price."

"We will have to deploy security to Norway but security is over stretched now, as they have struck all over the world. I will not fail you."

With that he rung off and immediately punched in the number of Bob Crowe.

"Hi Bob, Adolfo here. Have you got anywhere in identifying the fourth person."

Bob replied with some optimism, "The authorities in Israel think it may be someone called Ishai, one of their top majors in the Israeli army. He seems to have gone missing, but they cannot be sure, as he lost his wife to a suicide bomber and maybe hiding through depression or something like that. However he is an expert in weapons so would fit the bill perfectly. He has many contacts world wide and that would come in handy for buying drones and micro-Uzis which they have used so far. But it is disturbing this statement about Norway. The last thing we want is for their premier to be assassinated too."

"We will have to watch the Norwegian whaling ports like we are the Japanese but having said that they could be anywhere plotting anything."

"Yes I agree. This Sonny Preston is too clever for his own good and his friends in the computer and finance world will have to pay as well. He seems to have recruited well and he must have planed all of this ever since he was incarcerated in that Psychiatric Institute. The Israelis however do not want a scandal involving one of their finest and they are reluctant to send over a copy of a photograph but we are working on it. They find it hard to believe that one of their best should get involved with saving the whale."

"It explains much though, with the military expertise carried out so far. I mean those assassinations must have taken a supreme eye and the weapon involved must have been state of the art."

"Yes, we never did discover the weapon that they used but the fact that they have used micro –Uzis hint of an Israeli connection."

"So what are the Israelis going to do?" asked Adolfo.

"Their top brass are having a meeting. They do not want Israel to get dragged into an international terrorist plot. They like to keep their security issues low key. Besides they have enough on their plate with all the crisis in the middle east."

"Well I hope that they fully cooperate. It maybe that the death of this Ishai's wife has tipped him over the edge. It is just that they seem to be so well organised with insider help."

Bob Crowe replied, "They will make a mistake eventually and we will be ready to pounce. The trouble is they have caused carnage world wide already. All that talk of the 'World Caliphate' was a deception which got us looking at different angles. My gut instinct is that the Japanese whaling ports will be the next target but we, of course, cannot be sure."

"I guess all we can do is wait and see if their cover is blown. You never know someone may talk. Someone must know of their whereabouts. We have put a massive reward out for any information so you'd think that someone would betray them."

"These environmentalists all stick together for their cause. Personally I believe the underground green movement have been keeping them out of the picture. He is well versed is this Sonny Preston in how people think.

Well, it is the end of February so only another month to go before the fleet sets sail. I am sure that they will make a move before then. I don't envisage anymore daring attacks like the one on the emperor. But then again Norway could equally be involved. It was rotten luck on Tanya being freed by the court and of our losing contact. She was an expert at avoiding a tail. We had her under surveillance but she simply vanished. I wonder if she has met up with the other three and is calmly waiting for the next stage of their plans. But we could not touch her for the assassinations as she was not in Tokyo at the time. In fact we still don't know for sure that this gang of four exists. We have so little to go on, but we have a duty to protect the public and we can only hope that they make a mistake. The whole world is wanting to know what goes on inside one of these Japanese Scientific Whaling ships and I guess that we are about to find out in a month or so."

Adolfo remembered Suto's words about failure, and replied to Bob Crowe, "We will be waiting for them when they strike."

"I sincerely hope so. Well I will leave it there Adolfo. Keep me updated of any developments."

"Certainly will. Bye."

Adolfo disconnected the line and sat back in his chair and pondered on Sonny Preston, the man they had in their sights in Iceland. A lot had changed since then, and Adolfo was acutely aware that his reputation was on the line. He guessed that Sonny would know that he would be involved so it was a double edged blow.

CHAPTER 27

It was now the beginning of March 2016 and Sonny was finalising the communication with the administrator who was going to smuggle them on board a factory ship. But first he had some friends in Norway who were going to attack one of the whaling ports. He contacted them first and again was on a secure skype link. This meant that he could see whom he was chatting to over the computer's lap top.

"How's it going Brian?" asked Sonny. Brian Harding was the name of the contact in Norway who was going to explode a bomb in a Norwegian whaling port, called Barentsberg.

"It is all set for the 6th March, though I bet security will be tight due to your statement release. Even so I should be able to get through OK. I speak fluent Norwegian and can easily pass as a ship worker. How is it with you? Where are you?"

"We are in Japan about to hit the whaling port of Shimonoseki, and expose what is happening on these whaling ships in the name of science. We are soon to bribe an administrator responsible for recruiting workers to the ships. That will be in less than four weeks time."

"Sounds great. I wish you luck. Hopefully my diversion will take some of the heat off your port. How's it going with the security services chasing you?"

"We've been well catered for by the Japanese environmental movement. If only the government held the same views we would not have to do this. I will probably end up back in a psychiatric detention centre if I get caught," said Sonny with a touch of humour.

"As long as international whaling gets stopped that's what matters most, and the Norwegians are as bad as the Japanese. I intend blowing up one whaling ship which should be enough to bring the authorities to their senses. How's the rest of the gang? That Tanya was lucky to get off in court. Maybe it was a sign from God."

"We are all together now just waiting for the day the ships set sail to go hunting. We are finalising plans. Good luck with you Norwegian bombing. I will have to go before some security geek hacks in to our link."

"Thanks. Contact me on the 8th March to see how the world reacts."

"Will do. Bye for now."

The rest of the gang are pleased that Brian was carrying out the bombing on the 6th, but more especially they were wanting the day that they got smuggled aboard a Japanese Factory ship to arrive. Sonny said that now the tricky part was to come. Settling a price for the bribe of the administrator, who was called Horato Saki. They would need clothes as well to dress as Japanese fishermen. Ishai checked his explosives and micro-Uzis for the job and was pleased to report that all was well. Sonny e-mailed Horato and soon there was the return e-mail. As Sony had guessed the amount that the administrator wanted had gone up. Now it was ten million dollars. Although it was a sum he could afford it brought home the greed of mankind. Sonny wanted assurances that the sum would not go up again and that Horato could guarantee the smuggling aboard of the gang. He said it would not be a problem as the authorities trusted him and he was responsible for recruitment of the fishermen. Sonny said he would get 5 million dollars now and the rest after successful completion of the smuggling. He said the money would be transferred to a safe account for his collection. Horato gave Sonny the details of an account to which the money could be transferred and Sonny set the process in operation. The rest of the gang expressed a sigh of relief. They were almost there. Horato said that they would have to meet at night in warehouse number 15 by the docked ships so he could smuggle them on, so it was up to them how they got there.

Sonny consulted a map of the docks and saw warehouse number 15. He would have to tell Kuki to arrange the transportation. Horato said they could get dressed in fishermen's clothing there in the warehouse. He advised them that they were to say nothing, as he would do all the talking saying you were mercenary type people from Thailand eager to work on a Factory Ship as the pay was good. Sonny asked him which ship they would be going on and he was amazed when he said the Nishin Maru, the leading Factory ship.

Ishai said that he had already been aboard it and it was massive. How much luggage were they to bring knowing that the guns and explosives needed to be smuggled on board too. Horato said that quite a large amount of luggage could be brought. And they were expected to be away for 6 months. Horato thanked them for the 5 million dollars and said that he had to go and that they should keep in touch. He envisaged the 28th March as the night they would be smuggled aboard.

Sony ended the link and turned to Tanya. "So it is to be the Nishin Maru, the premier boat in the fleet. What you will have to do is make sure you look like a man when you dress as a fisherman. Do you think you can do that?"

"For a trip out on the Nishin Maru I can do anything. It should not be difficult if I put a bob hat on and glasses with a fake beard."

"Good thinking. We are almost there. We will need a plan when aboard. Do we mix with the crew of try and hide ourselves but bear in mind we could be at sea for weeks before they catch any whales."

"Yes, but we don't speak Japanese or indeed any other eastern language," said an excited Tanya.

Sonny replied, "Horato says many languages are spoken and not all the fishermen are Japanese. There are many different nationalities. It is just that generally speaking they will be on the look out for four people like us as it is all over the press and television not only the assassinations but that we may be targeting a whaling port. We have to hope that the Norway diversion puts them all off our trail. I could organise another diversion in which the gang gets captured by getting volunteers from Kuki's green movement to masquerade as us.

That would work as long as the volunteers knew the score. Kuki tells me that there are die hard Japanese greens who believe that whaling should stop, so it is a possibility. After all I am not convinced that the security apparatus has our gang worked out. They probably know that I have something to do with things but they have no proof or evidence that I am involved only a few scant pictures and that was not of us together. I will look into it. We will need to organise transport for the 28th March to warehouse number 15. Maybe a fish lorry will suffice as we don't want to arouse the suspicions of the authorities or security services. They must be fretting by now having got nowhere with the investigation into the assassinations. Sonny wondered how Adolfo was doing knowing that Sonny maybe involved but having no ability to catch him. Sonny always suspected that Adolfo was in the pay of Japanese business as to the nature of their relationship. Adolfo was obsessed with Sonny Preston. That was how it was. And it was dangerous. Sonny felt sure that Japanese big business was involved in Japanese whaling and that they would have their own type of security. Maybe they were watching them right now waiting to pounce.

CHAPTER 28

Sonny and the gang were glued to the television as reports came in of a bombing in the Norwegian whaling port of Barentsberg on the island of Spitzbergen. Journalists were asking the question of when these terrorists would be caught and brought to justice. Apparently one whaling ship had been targeted and blown to pieces, in what was quickly coming a mini war. It was now the sixth of March and Sonny hoped that this diversion would make the security services apply their over stretched resources to Norway. The Norwegian premier issued a statement saying no stone would be left unturned in our efforts to capture these terrorists. The whaling community were up in arms over the incident, saying the governments were not providing enough security. Surveillance cameras would have to be looked at. But it was dark at the time of the explosion so there would be difficulty in seeing anything of worth. Apparently Brian Harding had attached explosives to the outer hull which were detonated by telephone. He had quickly left the scene and drove away as quickly as he could. Then he switched cars a few miles away where he felt sure there were no security cameras. As Spitzbergen was an island he knew an abandoned airfield where he could fly off the island. He made the telephone call to detonate the explosives from the airfield. All was completed within hours of the explosion before the authorities could get organised. The plane landed in a disused airfield in northern Norway. He had made good his escape. He then drove all the way down to Oslo to merge in with the general population. He would get in touch with Sonny when ready and tell him all was well at his end.

Bob Crowe was on the line to Adolfo.

"Looks like they were telling the truth about Norway. They seem able to reach anywhere at any time. They are incredibly organised. Spitzbergen was an island so the authorities may have discovered the airfield that he escaped from. It is unlikely that the culprits would be hiding out on the island."

"It could be," said Adolfo," that they have friends in Norway who could carry out this bombing. I find it hard to believe that the four of them, if there are four of them, would do this act together. I think like you Bob that this may be a diversionary tactic to thrown us off the scent. That does not mean we are any nearer to finding them, only that we should not let down our security in other areas. But obviously we must investigate the Norwegian bombing thoroughly. But there are no pictures of them at sea ports or airports so how would they get about without being detected."

"I think that they are still lying low. After all what they did in Japan attracted a lot of attention. They must be afraid to surface or travel anywhere. They are obviously getting assistance from the Green movement's vast supporters. We seem unable to do anything. In fact we cannot do anything until we get sightings from the public or leads from our security services. But the fact remains the Japanese whaling fleet set sail at the end of March, so they should make a move before then. We've got to get our timing right and pounce about that time if our hunches are correct and that is what they are aiming for."

"We don't want to put all our eggs in to one basket. We cannot be certain that the Japanese whaling ports will be targeted. Shimonoseki has the Nishin Maru the main factory whaling ship. We will have security watch it, but let's be honest they could strike anywhere."

"I know, but we would look like fools if they struck and we were not prepared. The government are on our backs as we seem to be doing very little to capture these terrorists. They want action and there is an election coming up. Mary Simmons is not convinced that Sonny Preston was responsible for the assassinations. It is the work of someone with expert military training. Maybe there was leaked information from the police on the day of the murders saying where they would be and how they could be targeted. She feels that it may be some Japanese 'Red Brigade' type organisation such as the republican 'Soldiers of War' movement. They have made it their intention to kill the Emperor in the past. We are beginning to make this Sonny Preston like some supreme untouchable warrior. We have had little sightings and Tanya was cleared in court. We must not get over indulged with this Sonny Preston."

"In many ways you are right" said Adolfo." Mary Simmons is an expert in terrorism and if we look at the evidence all we have is a couple of grainy pictures and then they are not on the same picture. No one has seen anything until Tanya was picked up."

"Yes Adolfo, but they have not claimed responsibility and you would think that they would be bragging about it. After all it is quite a coup."

"Not necessarily. They have suffered losses to personnel in the past and may not wish to draw attention to themselves. If only we knew where Sonny Preston was we could sort the matter out. The fact that he has not come forward to help us with our enquiries says much. No, it maybe that the shooting of the Emperor and the Prime Minister was coincidental. We could be looking in totally the wrong place. Anyway we will watch over the Nishin Maru until it sails. There would be uproar if we advised the ships not to sail. They would think we were giving in to terrorism.

"OK, I will leave it with you Adolfo."

"Bye Bob" and Adolfo cut off the phone call.

Meanwhile, Sonny and co. were getting excited at their Nishin Maru project which was only a few weeks away.

"It's going to be tough getting aboard the Nishin Maru with suspected added security. It is probably being watched like a hawk. Just what have you got in mind Sonny?" asked Ishai.

"I'm relying on this administrator Horato to take care of that. He is likely to hold much sway in the scheme of things. I am sure he can come up with some story to cover his tracks. We will be arriving from here by a fish lorry to the docks. Probably it would be best if we were smuggled aboard two by two.

"Yes, but wont security be watching?" added Ishai somewhat confused.

"I am hoping that Horato can use his knowledge of the security workings to get around that. I mean he must know when there are shift changes and where the security are stationed. He probably knows how to knock out security cameras. Maybe he could smuggle us around the far side of the ship from the water's side and winch us aboard that way. That way we would be shielded from any form of security. It is certainly something we have to get right on the night. I will be in touch with Horato right up to the night we go for it.

"And what about when we are aboard?" asked Gustav.

"As I understand it we will be given cabins well down the ship. It is up to us how we plan our escapade. Obviously we will need to see some whales taken on board so that we can relay what they are doing to them to the world. And if we explode the ship we have to get off. That is where Greenpeace gets involved. As you are aware Greenpeace shadows the whaling fleet as it goes about its business. So at some point we will need to make contact and get transferred to the Rainbow Warrior.

"But what about food and the rest of the crew must surely spot us in our cabins. We cannot take all of our food supply with us. We will have to get access to the canteen on aboard the ship."

"Yes our plans our a bit flimsy at the moment but I will contact Horato, It maybe that we will be compromised by some of the crew or that someone can feed us from the crew. Money can achieve anything. Maybe we can stealth our way in to the canteen when it is closed and eat sandwiches. Maybe Horato can leave us with a big supply of food. It is not easy.

CHAPTER 29

Another week goes by and it is the 23rd March. One week before the fleet sails. Sonny was making contact with Horato and asked him about food and the rest of the crew. He replied that the cabins were well below deck and seldom used so it would be easy to hide there, but he had paid one of the crew to feed them should they need it as he would provide a supply of food in the cabins. Tins of meat and fish. Obviously that might not be enough so the crew member tasked with assisting them could provide bread. The crew member would be called Okai, and he spoke English. He was a bit cheesed off with the whaling fleet and its breaking of catch quotas so he would be good to have on board.

As Sonny was using his lap top to communicate with Horato he was unaware that Suto Suzuki and his expert computer team had finally managed to log in to the e-mail. This meant that Suto Suzuki had now knowledge of what they were going to do. So as Sonny kept on chatting to Horato, Suto became more aware of their plans. He realised that Horato had been bought off, but what was Suto Suzuki going to do now that he knew what the Sonny was up to and indeed had confirmation that they were the gang. He could tell Adolfo and Bob Crowe or he could, he deduced let their plan go ahead with his security team being on board. He wanted them dead whilst Adolfo wanted to obey the law. Eventually he learned that it was to be the Nishin Maru, the star of the fleet that they were going to attack and disrupt the whaling. They had only a week to go before Sonny boarded the Nishin Maru. Suto felt elated that he had got hold of the gang's plans. He could now take them out on the ship and be a hero to Japan. He knew that Sonny did not know who he was but he would have to tell the captain of the plans to let the four on board. He did not want Adoflo knowing, he decided as he was going to be a hero in taking out the gang. He thought that he would allow Sonny to see the whaling at first hand and then strike. He had lied when he had said to Adolfo that he did not know what was going on. He would allow Sonny to see for himself then strike him down. Sheer poetry.

Sonny was still e-mailing Horato when he got a call from Suzie Adams saying that his e-mail connection may have been compromised. It may be being listened to. Suzie Adams was an expert and said it was coming from Draxon pharmaceuticals. They obviously had an interest in the scheme of things. Sonny immediately logged off and told the others that they had probably been compromised.

Gustav was the first to talk, "So what now?"

"Well it looks like our plan has finally been discovered. The question is do we go ahead with our plans or abort. Suzie said it was agents from Draxon Pharmaceuticals so we do not know what to expect. Or what they are up to."

"Maybe we can e-mail them and offer another bribe," added Ishai.

"It is unlikely that a pharmaceutical company would allow itself to be bribed." Then Suzie Adams came on the line again and said that someone called Suto Suzuki was involved with the hack, so it would be wise to find out everything about him, which she was doing right now. It seems he is the chief executive officer of Draxon, but what will be his next move. "We can e-mail him and ask. After all we have put so much into our planning boarding the Nishin Maru maybe he will let us know what he has in stall. If he is in lead with the Japanese Whaling fleet he won't want compromising himself but will have secrets that he does not want out in the open. We could blackmail him by saying we are going to release a statement saying that his company is bound up with whaling. He is probably involved in illicit research on the poor beasts. Obviously he would not want the publicity.," said Sonny.

"Yes," said Gustav "that would work. But he may try and kill us whilst on the ship."

"We are prepared to die for our cause," said Tanya." But we have guns and explosives too. It would be hard to pull out of the operation now."

"People like him have tremendous egos. He is unlikely to tell Adolfo and his security team preferring to tackle us ourselves. I have a feeling that he will want to show us what the researchers are up to then kill us. If we are ready and prepared we can still overcome the odds. It is getting our explosives aboard and the Micro –Uzis. This Suto is bound to have a reception committee. We will wait a few hours and then e-mail him and see what he has to say. Suzie Adams gave him the e-mail address and Sonny, after waiting began the e-mail to Suto Suzuki. It started off by saying that if he went to the police we would tell the world that Draxon Pharmaceuticals was involved in experiments on whales aboard the Nishin Maru. Suto Suzuki realising that the e-mail was from Sonny Preston replied that they could come to some arrangement whereby they would both meet up on the ship and see for themselves the real nature of these experiments, if any. Obviously he did not want the good name of Draxon being tarnished world wide. It would effect sales of their many products. He added that he could call off security and meet them on the 28th March at the entrance to the Nishin Maru. Sonny turned round to face the other three and said what should they do.

"We.ve come this far. We should take up his offer though it will greatly affect their plans. We meet him and see for ourselves what is going on. What that will mean with the explosives and Micro –Uzis I don't know. He won't want us carrying those on to the ship. I think we can still smuggle those aboard by using Horato to winch them from the other side of the ship in berth. What bothers me is what the captain is going to think. I mean how are we going to hood wink him and his cabin crew. We are wanted throughout Japan." Said Gustav emphatically.

"Maybe if Suto said that we were researchers from America come to witness first hand the whaling. The captain is not to know that we are the gang responsible for the world wide atrocities. The captain is likely to do as Suto tells him. And if Suto vouches for us we could pull the wool over their eyes," replied Sonny.

"But surely because there would be four of us the coincidence would be obvious, especially with security telling the whaling fleet to be on the look out for anything extraordinary" replied Gustav. Remember Tanya was going to have to dress as a man."

"Yes, but if Suto Suzuki said that he could call off security maybe the ship and it s crew will think everything is fine. And maybe we could get friends in the green movement to come forward as the assassinators a few days before to throw the security team further from the trail. I will need to contact Kuki," Sonny tried to reassure Gustav.

Ishai said "It will be our last chance for over a year to infiltrate the whaling fleet. It may work or it may not but we have come so far to fail now. So I think we are agreed. Suto calls off security with some story about the four. We are now researchers for Draxon which Suto tells the Captain, and Kuki finds some volunteers to come forward for the assassinations. It is a long shot but once we set sail we are free of the landed security services. Remember Suto has large vested interests in the Whaling fleet. And his career maybe in jeopardy if he gets it wrong. If it goes well he could get a scoop saying how clean Japanese whaling really is. Maybe once we have left port Suto could come clean with the crew. It is all risky but we cannot afford to wait another year." They had only five more days in which to put their final plans into operation.

Sonny contacted Kuki with details of the deception and said there would be many willing volunteers wanting to claim responsibility for the murders of the Emperor and Prime Minister. They would issue a statement immediately.

It was all over the television and the radio when two people came forward saying the were from the 'Soldiers at War' faction that were republicans. This had nothing to do with whaling. They were fighting to rid the Japanese of this sycophantic Emperor Dynasty. Pressed on who strafed the Tokyo nightline they simply replied other volunteers.

They had been hiding in the vast Tokyo student underworld. They said the authorities had got it all wrong by saying Sonny Preston had a gang going round the world terrorising governments to stop whaling. He simply was not capable of doing such things and that the green movement were basically peace loving people.

Sonny and co. watched the television. They saw the two brave volunteers being arrested and brought to Tokyo central police station for questioning. What they hoped for now was a lessening of security over the fleet in Shimonoseki. They had five days to prepare for boarding the giant Nishin Maru. Meanwhile Suto Suzuki was making sure that the scientific experiments on the Nishin still went ahead as he wanted Sonny Preston to see them. The he was going to kill them and get the credit. Suto would tell the captain to keep on top of things in order to show this team of four researchers the harsh reality of research.

Adolfo was again on the telephone to Bob Crowe about these Soldiers at War duo coming forward and taking responsibility for the assassinations.

"Real turn up these two coming forward, Bob, I guess we can call off the security over at Shimonoseki."

Bob replied "Suto Suzuki the Chief Executive of the massive pharmaceutical giant Draxon has advised that security be scaled down now we've got these two. He says men from his company will keep a watch on the ships so we can call off our men. Men that could be employed better elsewhere."

Adolfo was astounded that Suto should get directly involved, but he knew that Suto thought him a bumbling idiot. What about his pension. If Suto solved the situation he probably would not be getting his pension and the fast cars that went with it.

Bob Crowe continued. "Anyway, if the chief executive of the Draxon thinks the fleet is safe then that is fine with me. Much ado about nothing, if you ask me. We've been giving this Sonny Preston too much man power and have been treating him like he is a superman. I never did think he was capable of shooting the Emperor. As for the other events we think he has carried out I personally still think it is a Muslim connection, largely because of the freemasons and the catholic church. So what if we have seen him with this 'mad dog Gustav'. He is not another superman. I will call off our security teams at the ports and see what happens with the trial of these two 'Soldiers at War' murderers. Mary Simmons felt that it maybe someone like that who could pull off the murders of the Emperor and the Prime Minister. They have enough hate in their hearts for the system."

"What if it proves to be another deception and that these two members of 'Soldiers at War' were put forward by the vast Greenpeace movement to take the blame?"

"Well, we will find out soon enough when they stand trial and they clearly have nothing to do with the Norwegian bomb."

"We cannot be everywhere and this Suto Suzuki feels that security can be scaled down at the port of Shimonoseki. It was probably wishful thinking that they would turn up there. If only we had more evidence that Sonny Preston was involved."

CHAPTER 30

It was the night of the boarding of the Nishin Maru for Sonny, Gustav, Ishai and Tanya. Tanya was dressed as a man with a beard and had to admit she did not look convincing as a man, but still she was passable. They got into the fish lorry outside their safe house and Ishai carried the bag of explosives and Micro –Uzis. The plastic explosives just need timer sticks to be implanted and a mobile phone could set off the explosion. They had to set off earlier than expected to get Horato to winch the bags aboard on the ocean side of the ship. He did not ask any questions and once the bags were on deck Ishai took them below. To where Horato said they would be. Then it was a question of hiding them in the cabin and then making his way back up to the top deck too meet up with Suto Suzuki. All in all it took five minutes of his time and no other crew members ask questions as he was with Horato. Suto met up with them at the end of the boarding plank and the ship was massive. They would be sailing the next day.

"Good evening," Suto said to the four as they arrived with Ishai slipping in from the back." I have told the captain that you four are guests of Draxon pharmaceuticals and will be observing the hunting of the whales. The Captain was against the idea at first but when I told him grants would be reduced if he did not comply he soon changed his mind. Security has been called off so we have nothing to worry about. Make yourself at home and don't worry about the crew as the Captain has briefed them that they have guests.

They had a few sparse bags with them for change of clothes but intended keeping a low profile until the ship made its first kill. Suto

187

did not trust their intentions and had back up security personnel on the ship, which Sonny suspected. Suto added,

"We should have our first kill in a few days. Then you can go down to the place where they cut up the meat and store it and see for yourselves what is going on."

Sonny shrewdly asked what Suto would be getting out of this saying that Sony and his associates have been already falsely accused of carrying out terrorist outrages. All Sonny wanted to see was what was going on after the supposed kills. Suto was exceedingly diplomatic, saying the Captain and his crew extend the hand of Japanese friendship. Suto was sure nothing untoward would be seen to be going on and after the trip maybe Greenpeace people would believe Sonny Preston version of events at having discovered nothing. They did not know that Suto had every intention of killing them at the first opportunity. Ishai was quick to mention to Sonny

"You cannot trust this guy. He may eventually kill us all."

"Yes I agree with you, but we have weapons. It seems that Suto is wanting to make a statement to the world and we are involved in that process. He wants to show the world that Draxon cares about whales and yet still his experiments will go on. He will probably hope to kill us after a few weeks at sea and take the credit for stopping our actions. In addition I must keep in touch with the Rainbow Warrior which is our way off the ship. We can get off via the slipway at the base of the ship. So it is a mere question of us blending in and with Tanya extra caution needs to be taken. We can well imagine a crew of randy sailors if they find a woman aboard, especially one as good looking as her.

The next day came and they set sail with Suto happy that the four were so easily tricked into his plan of action. Suto would contact the four when whales were brought aboard, and they could verify that internationally agreed quotas were being abided by. Suto guided them around the ship as Horato had not sailed with them. He would be wanting his other 5 million dollars. And Sonny even then did not trust him. Who could you trust in this situation? It took over an hour to see around the ship with its many rooms and refrigerators for the whale meat. All the while Ishai was taking it all in for places to put the explosives and exits and blocked paths. With a ship like this the crew work nights so he would have to be extra careful when he planted the explosives. But he had retained a map of the ship from when he worked as an undercover journalist and studied it carefully.

They were in their cabins and Sonny made the second payment to Horato and then contacted the Rainbow Warrior. Roger Smith the captain of the Rainbow Warrior said they would be tailing the Nishin Maru through the Sothern Oceans. It was noted that they would need their help in getting off the ship and they must keep in touch. The Southern Ocean was where the ship would be heading.

Okai brought them food and drink to their cabins. They desperately did not want to draw attention to themselves especially with Tanya dressed as a man. But they knew they would have to go into the canteen at some time. Suto was in his element. He had sailed with the fleet only once before but knew what was going on. He was going to let the gang of four know what experiments they were conducting and then dispose of them. He wanted to show his superiority in the scheme of things. But the first few days in to the voyage were nothing special. Sonny and his gang kept to themselves whilst the rest of the crew were quite jovial at their new year's voyage, singing songs and getting drunk.

Gustav was up late in his cabin and said to Sonny,

"What do you think this Suto is really up to? Why would he want to show us the experiments that we have suspected have been going on? It seems so strange that he should welcome us aboard with open arms."

"He is probably on an ego trip, thinking he can play God. Undoubtedly he is thinking of killing us after exposing the experiments. But what would the rest of the crew think. Four observers come to have a look themselves. You would have thought they would shut down the experiments. The secrets of them must be weighing Suto down and he is itching to share his importance with some one else. He seems to carry tremendous clout aboard the ship so we were right about Draxon being involved."

"So", said Ishai," What do we do now. Do you think we should wait until the ship successfully hoists some whales aboard because we must be on our guard for when Suto makes a strike against us which he surely will. He must have some security staff aboard for that purpose."

Sonny readily replied. "We do not need to stray much from our cabins during these early days. Okai can bring us food. By now everyone on the ship will know that we are here as a request from Suto, the big man. The crew will do as it is told by Suto. They will all probably think it is a big publicity stunt. But like you say we need to be ready for when he makes his move.

Tanya said "How were they going to do that. They could not walk around with Micro-Uzis in their hands and only Ishai was adept at one hand combat." Luckily she had done little talking yet so no one had suspected their little group. The general consensus was that Suto had invited them aboard and that Suto was the Big Man from Draxon, someone who paid for their fishing trips.

Tanya continued, "Chances are that Suto will come for us when we are sleeping rather than risk a confrontation in full view of the Captain and crew. He may try and drug our food for all we know.

Sonny quickly replied," Okai works for Horato so I doubt If he will drug our food. Besides we will have to take risks and start going the canteen. Maybe when it is not busy. But I agree Tanya he will probably come during the night when he expects us to be asleep. We will have to take it in turns to lie awake but nothing will happen until he has chosen to show us some experiments. And I guess what ever experiments they are will take some time to set up. I don't really know what to expect. We have always had our suspicions that horrific experiments are taking place but as of yet no one has found out. In that sense we are lucky to be on board. As son as we have witnessed what he is going to show us we take some pictures, relay them back to our sources and expose their racket and then lay the explosives and get off the ship. It is a lot to think about. Ishai, have you been thinking of where to lay the explosives."

"I have not had a good look around the ship yet but they will need to be laid for maximum effect, that is, to make the ship sink, so down below the water line would be a good place. I have to make sure that no one is about when I do it and that is not easy when there are so many crew. But I have a map of the internal drawings of the ship so should not get lost. With plastic explosives it is relatively simple. But it is a big ship. I am not happy with Suto though. He is surely going to try and kill us. If we could rig the explosives within the next few days before he shows us his grizzly experiments we could take the Micro-Uzis to the slip way and use them to negotiate our way off before Suto manages to come up with a plan to execute us. It would mean concealing them on the way down to the slip way and the room adjoining this. I will have to carry the bag but I think this is the wisest course of action else we could all be killed without a trace of the experiments reaching the wider environmental head quarters or the International Whaling Commission. The way I se it we have About 5 days before they harpoon any whales. Then deciding on what Suto says we have a window of possibly three days to learn about any experiments."

Sonny said, "Let's hope that they do not break the quotas rule and harpoon a Blue or a Humpback whale. These species are rare enough now. Chances are they will be the smaller Minke Whales. I think that they are allowed to take up to a thousand of these.

The next few days went uneventfully by with the Nishin Maru steaming its way to the Southern Ocean. It would not be long before some whales were harpooned and winched aboard by the slipway. Then Suto stopped by the Cabins of the gang of four saying that in a few days they were going to harpoon some Minke Whales. Suto had a gleam in his eye almost of a mad man come to gloat on some heinous act. As soon as we get word I will come and get you.

Ishai thought it a very good time to go and lay the explosives so he set off with map and bag saying he would be back within two hours at most. He went down into the depths of the ship looking for suitable places to lay the plastic explosives. It was important that the did not get caught as the whole operation would be compromised.

191

And he hoped that he did not get lost in the vast corridors of the ship. Maybe he should take Tanya or Gustav with him, but in the end decided against the idea. He thought he may come across some crew involved with the engine of the ship so he carried a gun just in case things got out of hand. But he imagined that in the main most of the crew would be playing cards in the canteen awaiting the first sightings of the Minke Whales which would be a few days off. Off he went into the dimly lit corridors of the ship. It would be twenty minutes before he again consulted the map and found himself on the bottom of the boat. All he had to do was locate the water line and apply the plastic explosives to the nooks and crannies of the metal hull. Then he heard voices and hid behind a metal projection while two people went by, no doubt on way to the engine room. When it was safe to come out he opened his bag and got to work with the explosives and pencil timers that the mobile phone would trigger off. All the while he was straining his ears for voices or noises of people coming along the bottom corridor of the ship. He decided that if he applied a little explosive well, there would not be any need to use the lot, as a major breech in the hull would do the trick. He did not like it down there on his own and was fearful that his torch would give him away. But all went well. He was back in his cabin in over an hour telling Sonny that all he needed to do was dial a number on his mobile and the hull would blow a hole. He could dial the number when aboard the Rainbow Warrior. He went on that he did not use the whole of the explosive as he felt that he may attract the attention of some of the crew.

"Good" said Sonny." We've just got to wait until Suto contacts us to go visit the slipway and the adjoining rooms where they carry out what ever they do. We need to keep the Micro – Uzis on us, under our coats. I don't know in his vanity whether Suto will bother to check us for weapons. As for cameras I don't know what he will think. He must know that if we record what we see by camera it will get out to the world's media. Maybe that is what he wants. To come clean. Maybe he is tired of all this secrecy and wants to end the speculation once and for all."

"Whatever he's doing he will want his company to do out in the open legally in the future to help justify the experiments," added Gustav soberly. "So our plan may backfire if the International Whaling Commission take his side in the affair."

"Well let's get some sleep," said Tanya. I will take first watch.

Meanwhile back on the mainland Horato had e-mailed Adolfo telling him that Sonny and his gang had somehow got on board the Nishin Maru though he was ignorant of their plans. Adolfo was fuming asking how it had been done. And Horato told him about Suto Suzuki. Bang went his pension he now thought but more importantly what was he to do now? Was he to tell Bob Crowe or let Suto Suzuki deal with them? Should he interfere, after all he was connected secretly to Suto and what would happen to him further should Bob Crowe find that out. He could let the authorities know anonymously. Maybe they could send helicopters out to track the Nishin Maru. Adolfo did not know himself what to do. In the end he decided to contact Suto directly to get his side of things. So he tried e-mailing him. Suto did not at first reply but then all of a sudden he received a reply to his e-mail.

"Don't worry Adolfo. I have it all planned out. Soon they will be dead. I have decided to let the gang of four see what exactly is going on then I will kill them. I have some security guards with me who have been briefed. It is best this way. I can kill two birds with one stone by hopefully letting the world and the International Whaling Commission know of any experiments that out great company has vested interests in."

Adolfo replied to his e-mail, "Do you want me to send some helicopters out in case things go wrong. We have contact with various Navy vessels throughout the seas who would lend us a hand."

Suto seemed annoyed at the suggestion. "Heavens no. We will deal with them here and now making my company heroes in the process. There is no need for helicopters or the like landing on deck. And the last thing I want is Bob Crowe and his ilk meddling in our affaires. We will have this all settled in a few days when we get our first whales on board."

"Ok Suto but don't forget my pension when you have sorted things out. I have been a good servant of yours over the years."

Suto cut off abruptly leaving Adolfo in a state of limbo over his beloved pension. He somehow had his doubts that the four would succumb that easily.

Adolfo got back to Horato asking what the aims of the four were. He said they simply wanted to know what was going on inside such a scientific research ship. And they had paid good money for the privilege. Adolfo asked Horato if he knew they were wanted terrorists. Horato said the evidence was flimsy and that two men had come forward for the killing of the Emperor and Prime Minister, and that they could not have done the Norwegian Bombing. He thought for the money they offered he could not refuse them a slot on the ship observing first hand any scientific research. And Suto Suzuki the big man from Draxon Pharmaceuticals had personally sanctioned the trip. If they are terrorists then it is their own fault for coming on board as Suto will have security guards ready to pounce. Horato said he felt that there would be no need to contact the governmental security services as Suto had everything planned. But Adolfo was not quite so sure feeling another international incident was brewing.

CHAPTER 31

Suto knocked on Sonny's cabin door to tell hi that some Minke whales had been sighted and that they were going to harpoon them shortly. This sickened Sonny to the core and he awoke the others to tell them to get ready. Stuff a Micro – Uzi up your jacket and have your cameras ready too. Sonny got out his lap top and contacted the Rainbow Warrior to tell them the news. Roger Smith replied that they were following the Nishin Maru towards a pod of Minke Whales. Did Sonny want them to disrupt the hunt or allow for several to be taken and winched aboard. Sonny said no matter how regretful they would have to allow the Nishin Maru to hoist aboard several Minke Whales to find out what was going on. They had no choice in the matter. Suto said that the Rainbow Warrior was hard on the Nishin Maru's tail and that they tried to stop the hunt with water cannon. Sonny and the other three followed Suto to the harpooning platform to witness first hand the plight of the Minke whales. Gustav felt like strafing the entire deck with the Uzi but managed to hold himself in check. Suto then explained that the initial harpoons just stunned the whales as they wanted them alive below deck. The precision harpooning made a swoosh in the daylight and blood could be seen in the waters. A winch hauled the harpooned whale up the slipway into the giant room at the centre of the ship. Suto told the four to follow him down below deck to see the next stage of the operation. This took some twenty minutes and Sonny noticed the extra security guards that Suto had employed on or around the slipway. A Minke whale was raised on a platform and doused with water as it was not dead. Some men were fastening a device to its head which Suto said was to measure brain activity. This was for Alzheimer's research. A hole was cut in its head for tubes to be put through. And wires were lead to a machine on the side of the room.

"Think about it Sonny," said an enraptured Suto," if Draxon makes a discovery that cures Dementia. Just think of the benefit to mankind and the money it will raise.

Ishai looked on like a true soldier knowing nothing could shock him, but Gustav and Tanya had turned pale with disgust. So this is what they were doing for scientific purposes finding a cure for Alzheimer's.

Sonny looked at the scene disgusted that creatures meant to play in the oceans of the world should end up having their brains dissected whilst alive. Gustav and Tanya got their cameras out and photographed the scene to relay to the Rainbow Warrior. Ishai then noticed the security guards of Suto get closer as if to attack so he got out his Uzi and strafed them all with the high powered velocity that is unique to the Uzi. Suto looked on crestfallen, then got his own gun out but Gustav successfully strafed him with his Uzi shouting,

"The Big Man falls." The remaining workers were rounded up and marched to a room by the side and locked in. They had to get off the ship and away from this ghastly sight. Sonny contacted the Rainbow Warrior telling it to come up by the slip way and to drop rafts to pick them up. This did not take long and when they were in the raft it was steered to the side of the Rainbow Warrior. The seas were not as choppy as they could be so all went quite smoothly. But by this time the crew on deck knew something had gone awry and they rushed down to the slipway room to see Suto dead along with his security guards. They freed the remaining crew members from the locked room. Once Sony and the rest of the gang were aboard the Rainbow Warrior they transmitted images of the Minke they had just seen back to Kuki and others in the Environmental movement. These pictures would prove dynamite to the International Whaling Commission who now had proof that experiments with no legal base were being conducted and that a total ban on whaling activities could now be asked for. Roger Smith and his crew felt they had made a significant breakthrough and that their work would be easier from now on. But there was the rest of the fleet to think of. Ishai just had to make the phone call to the ship timer sticks to set off an explosion to sink the ship of destruction. A loud explosion was heard and the ship began listing. They could see life rafts getting deployed on the top deck. The Captain was furious that his ship, his beloved Mishin Maru was going down. He swore he would get even with these gang of four who he now knew were the terrorists the world was looking for. He had half suspected they were not kosher but he had trusted Suto implicitly. He sent out SOS messages then he and his cabin crew got into the life rafts and lowered them over the side. Gustav and Tanya were cheering from the Rainbow Warrior and felt for that poor old Minke with its brain cut open in the name of research. Sonny asked Roger what he was going to do now.

"Well there's been a good job done there. We can either follow the rest of the fleet and stop them as best we can but I think after word of this gets about they will be recalled back to Japan. We need to call in to port so I guess New Zealand is the best place. No doubt we will get accused as usual of meddling in the internal affaires of Japan. What about you four? You are wanted from around the globe."

Sonny thought before he spoke. "I do not know what to do. I don't fancy going into hiding it could be I will give myself up. I think Whaling will be halted from now on now the I.W.C. know what scientific research means. I will have achieved my aim to stop whaling. The planet's seas will be free once more of the menace of the big whaling fleets."

Ishai said he would be returning to Israel to face the music. He said he was honoured to serve with Tanya and Gustav. He felt that Sonny if he gave himself up would end up back in a psychiatric institute. Tanya and Gustav did not know what to do. They expected a pardon for their efforts which they might conceivably get.

By now Adolfo and Bob Crowe had learned off the SOS from the Nishin Maru and of the deadly experiments being carried out upon it.

"Seems they were right all along about experiments being conducted aboard the Japanese Whaling Ships. It seems certain that whaling will be halted now," said Bob Crowe. As for the two men who came forward for the killing of the Emperor and the Prime Minister their trial is next week and we are no nearer to catching the Norwegian bomber. Reports are of four people who were invited on to the ship by Suto Suzuki escaping on to the Rainbow Warrior. Undoubtedly this was Sonny and his gang. They've got the news headlines again. Why Suto Suzuki should want to invite them aboard the Nishin Maru is anybody's guess."

"What we will have to do is track the Rainbow Warrior and arrest them when they dock in port." replied Adolfo who now had resigned himself to a retirement without an additional pension from Suto. "The rest of the Japanese Whaling Fleet has been recalled back to port, so it seems that this gang of four has been successful in that respect.

Bob Crowe thought it highly likely that the gang of four would claim political asylum. "Yes you are right we have to track the Rainbow Warrior. They were at the edge of the Southern Ocean when this happened so I have had to call in military intelligence to track them. There are military planes flying overhead now feeding us the position of the Rainbow Warrior. From all accounts it may be heading for New Zealand. It is mid April now and it may take them over 8 days to get there. It is a fast ship the Rainbow Warrior."

Adolfo interrupted," Bob, Sonny Preston is aboard the Rainbow Warrior, he has just issued a statement saying that he and his three associates will be claiming Political Asylum in New Zealand." Whilst he realises that he has done wrong with the terrorist atrocities carried out he now hopes an emergency meeting of the International Whaling Commission may halt all whaling, due to the four of them exposing experiments orchestrated by Draxon Pharmaceuticals into Alzheimer's Disease. Sonny Preston has shown that this ruse of Scientific Whaling is a trick to justify cruel experiments. We dread to think what other experiments are going on. It is the hope of Sonny Preston that all whaling will cease from now on, but we had to bring the issue to the attention of the world which we have done. We are confident that we will be granted Political Asylum to enable us to live a life free of retribution in New Zealand. The International Whaling Commission is calling a conference in a week's time to discuss these important issues. We have the support of Greenpeace and other environmental movements who although they themselves despise violence to achieving their aims believe that this gang of four will be seen as revolutionary in exposing the abuse of scientific whaling. Any halting of whaling is to be welcomed."

"This Sonny Preston has got a nerve" blasted Bob Crowe. After causing mayhem around the world, something we have had difficulty proving until now, he wants Political Asylum. Chances are he will get it too. We will be powerless to arrest them for their crimes."

"Seems like he has had everything worked out all along. He has had enormous assistance from some of his academic friends in computers in the States. We believe that Tanya is with them. She certainly tricked the Japanese court system. You've got to admire his planning even if you are his sworn enemy. He has issued this statement to the world saying that someone had to try and stop the genocide of the whale even if governments would not listen. Well they are listening now. He has not named the people in his gang but that will all come out in the Political Asylum claim. We can put up a good fight to stop his claim for Political Asylum saying that they are international terrorists responsible for murdering many people. Anyway Bob, all we can do now is wait until they dock in New Zealand which gives us 7 or 8 days to plan a strategy to prevent their Asylum claim. But I agree with you they will probably get granted Political Asylum. Where they will live then is anybody's guess. I will get back in touch with you when they dock in New Zealand. Bye."

"Bye Adolfo," said Bob Crowe." It is a pity that this Suto Suzuki intervened when he did. We were watching the Whaling ships at Shimonoseki and could have arrested them if he had not scaled down security. I bet they had inside help there anyhow. Too late now."

CHAPTER 32

The Rainbow Warrior made its way to New Zealand with Sonny Preston and his three friends treated with real respect by the crew. They had done what the Rainbow Warrior had always feared to do by blowing up the Japanese Whaling fleet's leading ship. The gang of four ate and slept well and were tired from their ordeals. Next step would to get the government of New Zealns to grant them Asylum. New Zealand was very against Whaling so it should be a done thing.

The trial of the two men who Kuki said had volunteered to stand trail for the murder of the Emperor and Prime Minister of Japan was going ahead on the 20th April. Sonny Preston wondered what they would do now that the ruse to take the pressure of the gang had worked. He would not like these two innocents to go down for a crime they did not commit. And he got his answer that morning as it was announced that the two men had withdrawn their statements of having killed the Emperor and Prime Minister. They said they did not do it. The case for the prosecution collapsed leaving the real culprits still at large. But the world knew that Sonny Preston and his gang of three had carried out the killings and the rest of the atrocities. It may not work for their attempt at Asylum but he felt he had achieved his goal of total whaling cessation, and his mood was one of jubilance. Tanya, Gustav and Ishai were also over the moon that whaling should cease from now on, Gustav was especially elated. Ishai knew for certain that when they claimed for Asylum on docking in Christchurch South Island, that he would be named to the world. He felt strange for having carried out so much with military precision

in secret he would now be famous across the world. What would the
authorities think of him in Israel, where he had once a wife. Would
it ruin the reputation of Israel? Many such questions went through
his mind. But he felt as if he had done the world a favour. For sure
the world's many environmentalists would see him as a hero. He
recalled seeing that Minke whale with its head open with tubes
poking out. The whale that had never harmed man, that had simply
swan in the seas for eternity allowed once more to swim freely. He
recalled the eulogies of Sonny that persuaded him to join this mission
and felt it was a job well done, no matter whether they were granted
Asylum or not. Gustav seemed not to care too much what happened
to them so elated was he at having found out what the Japanese got
up to with their scientific research. He shuddered at just what else
they may have been getting up to. Finding a cure for Alzheimer's
Disease the tip of the Iceberg. He realised that people had died but
felt it was all in a good cause. He would go back to Germany a hero
too. Tanya who by now had got rid of her disguise as a man felt her
life now had achieved something. All that going on marches to save
the whale meant something. They had dared to take on the world's
governments and were a stone's throw away from being granted
Political Asylum. She thought of Sonny Preston a man she had met at
the Icelandic Whaling Conference and how his vision had come true.
The emergency session of the international whaling conference which
meets when they were about to dock in New Zealand will surely call
a complete halt to whaling. No more would countries be able to hide
behind the ruse of scientific whaling. That would be gone forever.

Would the four get granted Political Asylum after some very
serious terrorist incidents? The position of New Zealand was one
of fierce anti whaling and the four had demonstrated that scientific
research was going on these Factory Whaling ships. It would be
difficult to back up their case and New Zealand would be under
pressure from other countries not to grant them Asylum. They were
a mere few days away from New Zealand and no doubt Adolfo and
company would be waiting for them. Sonny did not fancy spending
the rest of his days in Prison. He wanted to be free as the whales

they had just saved. He knew that Samoa did not have an extradition treaty with the gang of four's countries and that Samoa was not far away from New Zealand. Maybe he should divert to Samoa and claim Political Asylum there. What did the others think? None of them had given much attention to capture but they could not be captured on Samoa. Sonny spoke with the Rainbow's captain Roger Smith, saying that he felt they had better chances with as regards getting freedom if they headed for Samoa. Roger Smith said it was no problem heading for Samoa. He agreed with Sony that it was a long shot if New Zealand granted them Political Asylum whilst on the other hand they could stay in Samoa for as long as they wanted. So the four agreed to head for Samoa. The would be there in two days. They knew nothing about Samoa but figured the climate would be okay.

In two days time the Rainbow Warrior manoeuvred into the port of Apia and Roger Smith let the authorities know that they had four people aboard who were claiming political asylum. Adolfo and Bob Crowe had been waiting in New Zealand as they had been lead to believe that the Rainbow Warrior was heading there. They were furious when they found out they had made for Samoa. There was no extradition treaty there and they would be granted Political Asylum much to their dismay. They realised that they had carried out some quite awful acts but knew that in their hearts it was worth it to stop whaling. Sonny was going to issue a statement to the world and it was the International Whaling Conference Emergency meeting the next day,

Sonny's statement went as follows.

"We four humble people have had a dream to prevent the world wiping out the whale. We got sick of governments allowing various countries to whale for scientific reasons. So we decided to do something about it. In September last year we attacked the Christ the Redeemer Statue in Brazil. Brazil an apt target as their government is allowing for the destruction of rainforests for ranches to rear cattle for MacDonald's. We then took out a freemason lodge in Germany knowing just how important the freemason were to the world. We then organised a bombing of the Longchamps race course in Paris on October. We were determined to get out message over to the governments of the world. For too long has the green environmental movement been pacifist and we knew that if we wanted whaling to halt substantial actions had to take place. We then killed an Indian Industrialist who owned a pharmaceutical and pesticide company. But lastly as Japan has been the leading nation connected to whaling we took out the Emperor and Prime Minister of Japan. We felt that this would awaken the government to the fact that we meant business. We have had substantial help from top academics in America who could hack into the world's security computers which enabled us to go undetected for so long. However it was our final act of sabotage that we are most proud of. Exposing scientific experiments on a Japanese Factory Ship. It seems that the chief Executive Officer of Draxon Pharmaceuticals of Japan, a certain Suto Suzuki was in lead with these experiments. We relayed pictures of these back to various governments and there will be an emergency session of the International Whaling Commission tomorrow in London to discuss all of this. We then blew the ship up after Suto Suzuki got killed whilst producing a gun. He seemed so keen to let us know what was going on, no doubt secure that he could kill the four of us. But his plan backfired and we are now here today at the end of April in Samoa where we will be granted Political Asylum. It is just a formality. There will be some nations dismayed at our Political Asylum but we can play the system too as much as scientific whaling used to play the game. We wait until tomorrow for the emergency session of the I.W.C. We are four simple people, namely Sonny Preston, Tanya Brown, Gustav and Ishai from Israel who have made history."

A governmental official boarded the ship and confirmed that the four had been granted political asylum and that they were free to do whatever they wanted to. There was no extradition treaty with the United States or Canada or Germany or Israel. The four of them did not know what to do at first, as now they were exposed and they would have made many enemies world wide.

"We can either stay here on the boat or go into town and book into a hotel" said Sonny to the others." I am not too sure what Political Asylum means in its entirety but I think we have the run of the country and as long as we don't break any laws here we can stay as long as we want. And I think we will be staying for quite some time, maybe forever."

"I would love to go back to Israel" said Ishai but I don't know if that is possible. We will have to enquire as to what we can or cannot do."

"I've got my dogs in Canada" added Tanya "But maybe they can join me over here."

"I will miss Germany" said Gustav "Yet it has been a pleasure working with you people."

"We will just have to wait for the I.W.C. emergency session tomorrow and see what they say but we are now famous in the annals of anti- whaling movements," said Sonny. "Let's stay the night aboard the ship and party with the crew. We don't want to bump into Adolfo or any of the security apparatus that has been chasing us for so long. We should have mentioned this to that governmental official as I am sure that they could arrange for a guard for us. We must be viewed from now on as Political Refugees needing protection. We want the I.W.C. to announce to the world our Political Asylum tomorrow so that we can lead as best a life that is possible. Ishai says he wants to go back to Israel where he will probably be court marshalled. I don't know if he will be a hero in Israel but to many in the green movement he will be. The trouble is if we return to our countries of origin another country may try and extradite us.

The next day came around and they turned on the television on the ship to watch the proceedings of the I.W.C.

"Friends" said a spokesman, "We convene here today in an emergency setting to discuss the activities of Sonny Preston and his gang. As you may be aware they exposed illegal research experiments aboard the Nishin Maru Factory Whaling ship of Japan. We are vehemently against such things. It seems that the Japanese authorities have been pulling the wool over our eyes about scientific whaling and that the same is likely with the Norwegian fleets. The term scientific whaling was meant to be a science about sizes of whales and weights not research into Alzheimer's disease. The commission takes its responsibilities very seriously and takes the stand that all whaling must from now on cease. Whether it will resume again depends upon the countries concerned. We know that Sonny Preston has caused mayhem among the world with his terrorism and that the aim of his gang has always been to stop whaling. Well they have achieved that, as the commission was unanimous in its condemnation of the Japanese research. Also it condemned the manner in which Sonny Preston set about his tactics to stop whaling, going further and stating that the commission was ardently against terrorism in all its forms. But circumstances had made an emergency session possible. The commission understands that the four have claimed successfully Political Asylum in Samoa, saying their crimes are politically motivated so the commission cannot recommend the four being arrested. From the 8th of May we declare that all international whaling cease and that if this endorsement is broken action will be taken against the country concerned. The I.W.C. will meet every 6 months from thence to discuss the results of the ban."

Whilst watching the television monitor the four were jubilant. They had achieved their aims to stop whaling and the commission said the ban was indefinite. The whole mood of the Rainbow Warrior was of elation with much cheering. Adolfo and Bob Crowe were in Samoa in the vain hope of arresting the four but of course they were not allowed to do this.

"Just think of the victims of his crimes and the many casualties and they get Political Asylum," said an outraged Bob." There must be something we can do.

Adolfo added "We can petition the authorities saying they are wanted terrorists with blood on their hands. Trouble is countries like Samoa want to keep their neutrality. We cannot extradite them as Samoa is a non extradition treaty country. So until they leave and go to a country where we can arrest them they are free to do whatever they like. If only we had prosecuted Tanya successfully in Japan. We may have got all four of them then. But Suto Suzuki brought his own downfall by allowing them on the Nishin Maru. He underestimated their zeal and cunning. We would have surely arrested them then as we were watching the ships for crew to be taken on board. Anything untoward would have bee noticed by our security services. Now all the Pharmaceutical companies that were testing new products on the whales are banned from whaling. In some ways I agree with this ban. I don't see how research on a whale can assist human beings. It smacks of sadism. Still that does not mean that any have a go hero terrorist can blow up half the world trying to stop whaling. They have got away with it but will probably have to live in Samoa for quite along time yet."

And so there you have it. Four dedicated lovers of the whale bringing about the cessation of whaling. Hopefully it would be forever, but if not who was to say that these band of four would take to the oceans yet again. Tanya brought her dogs over and had a big chat with her parents by phone. They seemed very alarmed at the behaviour of their daughter, whom they always thought a pacifist green. They never did catch the sadists behind the dog murders in Canada though the authorities felt it may have been something to do with pharmaceutical research. Tanya to this day thought it may have been Suto Suzuki trying to scare Tanya for meeting with Sonny Preston at the Icelandic I.W.C..

Printed in the United States
By Bookmasters